SEAMUS KEENAN

———

ABOVE THE CLOUDS
AND A DUTCH AUCTION

Published by Keenan Publishing 2006

Copyright © Seamus Keenan, 2006
All rights reserved

Printed and bound in Ireland by
Colour Books Ltd., Dublin
Set in Garamond

Cover Design by Paul Donaghy

This book is sold subject to the condition that it shall not, by way of trade or otherwise, be lent, resold, hired out, or otherwise circulated without the publisher's prior consent in any form of binding or cover other than that in which it is published and without a similar condition including this condition being imposed upon the subsequent purchaser

ISBN 978-0-9552827-0-6

Above the Clouds

1

One late summer's day when Sean was about thirteen years old, Stevie Bloomfield painted the front door of the family house a dark green colour. The letter box, knocker and numerals five and four he painted black from a small lacquer tin, and all under the admiring gaze of a fair haired boy. His silky flourishes, running commentary and swaying body belied the fact that he was far from sober. Not that Sean was aware of his condition, as far as he was concerned this was a first class job of work, performed by a master craftsman.

'Away in young fella,' Stevie drawled, 'and get your mother to come out here to see a fine bit of work.'

Sean loved the shape and the detail of the door, though strictly speaking the family didn't own the door or the house. It belonged to his widowed grandmother. But when the door was snibbed shut the hallway to the house proper was as safe as the Berlin wall. He was immune or so he thought from all danger – marauding savages, drunken rustlers or Chinese communists. Hopalong Cassidy the famous cowboy would gallop up and down the narrow mesa with guns ablaze, ducking and diving the arrows fired at him from the stairway bluffs by the Apache braves. Cochese the great Indian chief was acted by another friend of his, Jeff Chandler.

'How's Stevie getting on with the door?' queried Sean's mother, her lilty west Cork accent resonating from the back of the scullery. It seemed a rhetorical kind of question so the boy didn't answer.

General house maintenance was left to the mother of the house. His father never bothered himself with such mundane matters, as he had more important things to occupy his mind. He would spend hours fixing the wire muzzles for the greyhounds, of which he had many, or just bending wire into fantastic little animal shapes. Away from the racetrack the dogs were gentle streamlined beautiful creatures. Fleet of foot these hounds of Ulster who had hunted with Cuchulain and the Fianna galloped up and over O'Brien's hill and around the fields of Mullaghadun and Glenadush where unsuspecting hares with quivering ears nibbled the lush clover. Millions of years earlier, beyond the Ice Age dinosaurs had roamed and roared in these very fields.

In reality very few repairs were ever carried out to what was a rambling three-storey Victorian town house, with a high walled concrete yard and squared-off whitewashed stone out-buildings.

Above the Clouds

Painting and wallpapering of various rooms was undertaken at infrequent intervals. The arrival on holiday of two of Sean's aunts from Boston in America provoked a flurry of activity. That summer all the windows in the house received a coat of white paint, woodwork in the hall and landing was varnished or re-stained and many of the walls were repapered with floral patterns and prints that looked very similar to that which was removed.

That autumn an American cousin called Freddie White came to the house. He was a private first class in the navy and his uniform was a dazzling white which matched his teeth. His battle cruiser called the USS Atlanta which had docked in the Foyle estuary was a pale grey colour with white markings.

The wallpaper in the boxy bedroom which Sean shared with his twin brother Eddie, had bunches of blushing flowers printed all over it at regular intervals, and the ceiling which ran down at an angle to meet an iron-framed window was painted a sky blue. The finger of the windows jammed catch pointed out and away to the shimmering saucer of the Black Lough. Beyond the wavy brick and concrete border of the town the Lough floated among cattle-dotted fields and rushy meadows, and west of it lay the Indian reservation clustered with painted wigwams. Further west still lay the great plains and the Little Big Horn, Wounded Knee, Fort Baxter and the Seventh cavalry, and the Indian nations of the Sioux, Apache, Blackfoot and Pawnee. One day, Sean's father told him that Hughie-the-root Donnelly had been born on the little island in the middle of the Lough.

Sometimes at night moonlight spilled through the window panes and along the linoleum floor as far as the base of the demoralized wardrobe like the tide that left its high water mark on a harbour wall. Sean's bed was beside the door and opposite it was the identical iron-framed bedstead of his brother and on the sloping ceiling above them hung balsa-wood model aeroplanes, including a Focke-Wolf tri-plane with a six foot wing span.

After the rosary was finished in the sitting room downstairs the twins climbed the wooden hill to bed with the words 'night, night, sleep tight' from their mother. The boys would answer, 'night, night', in harmony, and prepare themselves for the nocturnal visit of snorting dragons, white unicorns and fierce rats. In the darkness the bedroom soon filled up with clanking shapes, jostling shadows, spidery men in swallow-tailed coats and battered top hats, wonderful wizards, diamond eyed snow queens and one-legged soldiers.

In the pitch darkness of a cold night the twins would settle down in their beds and sing aloud the songs they heard their father sing, Irish ballads like The Wild Colonial Boy, Boulavogue, Galway Bay, The Bard of Armagh, and his favourite The Minstral Boy... Then came the Western Cowboy songs like The Strawberry Roan, El Paso and There's a bridle hanging on the wall ...

'There's a bridle hanging on the wall
And a saddle in an empty stall

Above the Clouds

There's a horse shoe nailed upon a door
It's a shoe that my old pony wore
No more he'll answer to my call
And his bridle's hanging on the wall'

Sometimes he strummed a guitar or played on an old fiddle, but the coming of the television put an end to that. 'Bye-bye baby, baby good-bye', he would sing. Sean knew for certain that this man was his real father, a man with brylcreamed hair that he called dad. Once when he bust into the downstairs lavatory at the back kitchen he saw his father peeing and was astonished at the size of his willie. It looked like a gigantic red cucumber, but confirmed for Sean if proof were needed that this definitely was his father.

The green front door opened on to Scotch Street and like the grand old duke of York's men it was either half way up or half way down the hilly street. From the market square at the top of the hill the shops and dwelling houses spilled all the way down in a straight line for about three hundred yards, over the metal bridge into Beechvalley and the train station.

'All change, all change, for Omagh, Strabane and Derry', shouted Wilfie Wright the station master and blew his whistle. Two short shrill blasts were followed by a longer lingering note, a declaration of both authority and subservience from a man in a uniform belonging to the Great Northern Railway Company. On wash days Sean's mother would listen for the sound of the eleven o'clock train to Belfast – too loud a hoot and she knew that rain was in the wind and the clothes were hung inside.

'Chuffies coming down the track, down the track, down the track. Chuffies coming down the track, when's he coming back?' went the rhyme, and the iron horse snorted across the prairie lands of Kansas and Oklahoma feasting on the buffalo.

Directly opposite and set back from the street line stood the baronial stone bulk of the Presbyterian church. Every Saturday morning during the summer months old Bob McGilly sat on the pavement beside the entrance railings and closed his eyes. Settled down on a greasy overcoat he would play on a battered and bandaged melodeon. Filthy strips of sticking plaster were all that held the gaping sections of the instrument together, as timeless and forlorn notes were squeezed out into the breeze in the hope of separating a few coppers from passing housewives or sympathetic shop-keepers. From his vantage point at number fifty four Sean watched a street artist whose lack of musical talent never prevented him from amassing a pile of pennies, halfpennies and the odd threepenny bit during his morning sojurn. The church of the Volunteers which had been convulsed in times passed by protests and the sounds of marching bands was now obliged to listen to the unmelodic notes of a dreamy tramp. The stringed melodies from the great Carolan's harp never reached the tufty ears of old McGillie.

Above the Clouds

Sean's mother eyed the freshly painted door up and down for a few seconds before she spoke.

'What's wrong with the frame and the surrounds?'
'What's wrong with them?' queried Stevie.
'Sure they need lick of paint as well', she said, her voice tailing off a little as a pained expression appeared on Stevie's ravaged countenance. He swayed a little and removing the butt of a cigarette from his lips with nicotine stained fingers he snigged it out with a deft movement. To the observant teenager he looked for all the world like Fred MacMurray in the film Double Endemnity but without the soft hat.

'Can't paint without paint Ma'am', he replied with the ghost of an American accent, fixing his gaze on Sean. Then he coughed a long rasping cough and his maleness somehow disappeared under the stern look of the housewife.
'The tin's nearly empty', he said meekly, prodding with his right shoe the tin which sat on a folded newspaper.
'I gave you money for a big tin so I did. Sure that's not a big tin', she replied, and bending down she lifted the tin up, paper and all, and thrust it to within a few inches of Stevie's prominent nose.
'Is it?', she demanded.
His arms sort of fell to the sides of his splattered dungarees, his eyelids drooped and his lower lip just hung there. Sean felt embarrassed.
'I suppose you drank the half of the money I gave you in Stewarts' pub, and then thinned the paint with turpentine', she sighed.

Sean remembered the words of another song his father had sung,
'Cigarettes and whiskey and wild, wild women,
They'll drive you crazy they'll drive you insane'.

His mother's next remark was unexpected.
'Come in to the house so, and I'll make you a cup of tea', and turning to Sean she said,
'Your father will be back soon and he'll give you money to go down to Vinnie Quinn's for another tin of gloss paint'.

    Stevie's place was taken by Johnny McGirr, a general handyman who finished the job but left drops of dark green paint all over the pavement by the door. A few months later Sean's mother came in from the front door saying, 'That was the baul Stevie ringing at the bell, and him well oiled. He asked me for a bob for a sandwich, so I said to him, show me the sandwich first.'
    Sean knew neither of his grandfathers. His father's dad, called James had dropped dead in the market yard surrounded by cattle dealers, farmers and tanglers. The body was carried the short

Above the Clouds

distance up the steep hill to the house, on a door wrenched from an outhouse in the yard. As Sean was only about two years old he remembered nothing of the episode but in a family photograph saw himself sitting on the knee of a bowler-hatted man with a white moustache.

Hundreds of years earlier the Holy Roman Emperor Charlemagne wept when his commander La Chasm de Roland, the conqueror of the Moors was carried from a battlefield on the shields of his comrades. The boy began to disentangle himself from the family roots that held him in the fields of rickety haystacks and lanes of horse manure. Soon after his grandmother took to the bed.

Sean's father, John came back from his milk round about twelve o'clock with a surly darkening of unshaved skin about his chin and jaws, his double, Humphrey Bogart was starring in a movie about Africa. He sat down to a hard boiled egg, tea and toast at the table in the kitchen. This was his tiny mountain-top kingdom, his snow-capped Nepal and outside, the walls of the yard got higher and higher. In the dead of night he supervised the construction of the wall. Hoards of coolies clambered up the north face, each carrying on his back a heart breaking stone that had been smoothed and rounded by rivers of ice. One morning he looked up and in the great blue yonder he saw a gigantic mushroom cloud begin to form, a spectacle that was seen all the way to Christmas Island in the Pacific ocean, and even as far away as Dienbienphu in distant Indo-China.

A saucepan full of eggs was hard boiled every few days for an aviary full of prize winning canaries. The shelled eggs which formed an essential part of their diet were pressed through a wire sieve using the back of a spoon. Then a couple of Marie biscuits were pulverised between the sheets of a newspaper with a wooden rolling pin. The crumbs and egg were mixed with a little sweet milk and fed to the birds twice a day. The aviary itself was a wooden-framed lean-to about six feet by ten feet which jutted out into the yard between the sitting room window and the kitchen window. It had a sloping felt roof, low level wooden panels and was sheeted all round with fine netting wire. The birds, Yorkshire rollers and yellow borderers were kept primarily for their singing and not for their plumage.

To the watchful boy the best singing bird of all was the pink mule, a cross between a canary and a goldfinch. He thrilled to the sound coming from the throat of these sterile hybrids as did the busmen, bank managers, solicitors and others who came into the yard enthralled by the majesty of the music. Even in the depths of winter when icicles slipped over the precipitous edge of the aviary to hang down in long silver spears, the canaries still sang. In the piercing cold they knew that survival depended on their ability to fly endlessly from branch to perch to nesting box and back again. In the yard the singing birds put time on hold, and at first light their inflatable song filled the air and swelled like a giant balloon up into the atmosphere above the great wall.

This early morning recital was often interrupted by the sleepy persistent barking of Sandy the faithful yard dog. Sandy was of mixed pedigree, mostly corgi, and was known and feared in the

Above the Clouds

street for his unpredictability and ferocious temper. Sean regarded him as one of the family yet the dog knew his place in the order of things. He would lie outstretched in front of the kitchen fire of an evening but always moved without a murmur to accommodate the chair legs and feet of his human benefactors. At regular intervals during the day the dog would patrol the perimeter of his territory with military precision. Out through the front door he trotted on short legs, on his tour of inspection, pausing to check both up and down the street for the presence of any stray animals. A sustained high pitched bark was usually enough to frighten away any unfortunate canines. Past McIvor's drapery shop he would sail sometimes breezing as far down as Jim Reid's sweet shop before wheeling back up the hill again. Sandy would then sit on his hind legs for a while before sniffing his way up to the big gate and into the yard proper. Like most houses in the street the entry fronted a wide carriage arch which in years past would have echoed to the clip clop of horses hooves as carts trundled in and out. An old horse collar and harness still hung down from the rafters in the hay loft at the far end of the yard.

   Joe Weir used to deliver parcels around the town for the railway company on a flat wagon drawn by a black horse with a white blaze stamped on its forehead. The four wheeled wagon was painted a deep maroon colour, the same as the railway station, and the name Great Northern Railway was hand painted in black and gold lettering along its length. The thirteen year old boy marvelled at the sign writer's skill, and wondered if Stevie Bloomfield had painted it.

   From the yard Sandy skipped down a narrow alleyway which cut through a two-storey block of out-houses positioned at right angles to the house, into another high walled sloping yard. Open, empty cattle sheds flanked each wall and below that a brick byre with concrete stalls, and then a small gate led to the dairy and red hay shed. Next to this stoney fortress the land spread itself out like torn patches of fields, pasture, orchard and garden sewn together with threads of hedgerow and gravely paths. Beyond this family domain stretched the pearly peak of the far pavilions and the rainbow gold of the Sierra Madre mountains. Out there also on its stone pyramid stood the milky summit of Everest where Edmund Hillary and Sherpa Tensing had stood triumphant in the glistening sunshine.

   Sandy never ventured into the unknown south beyond the security of his stone pale. Not for him the haphazard spaces and scattered settlements of an endless panhandle. From the safety of the stockade his gaze was never puzzled by the trails of smoke on the horizon or by the whisperings carried on the warm winds which blew across the great pampas beyond the shining river. His only torment in an otherwise idyllic existence came from a pure bred cocker spaniel bitch which belonged to Sean's next door neighbours.

   The Stevenson's neatly tended garden with its pale blue rhododendron bushes occupied a long rectangle of ground on the other side of the wall directly opposite the tarred cow sheds. Alan Stevenson was a quiet vet, the second husband of a big boned Gilford widow whose family were owners of a linen mill. Due to the steep gradient of the street their house, number fifty two, had three stone steps with a black iron hand rail leading up to the front door. The heavy

Above the Clouds

panelled door boxed around with glazed side and top sections was protected from the elements by a decorated porch of carved scrolls and a sand-stone pediment. A polished brass plate identified the owner by name and profession. Though the Stevenson's had two girls about Sean's age he never saw inside the house nor was he ever curious about its contents, but he was impressed by their grandiose door compared to his.

Their spaniel, known as Kerrigan, had for days on end barked incessantly down at Sandy from the relative safety of the high dividing wall. Sandy, for his part, just ignored the nuisance from above and bided his time. One wet afternoon the doorbell rang, followed by an impatient staccato knocking. In the half opened doorway Mrs Stevenson's bulky frame quivered like an enormous jelly, obliterating the daylight and throwing a black shadowy veil over the figure of Sean.

'It's Kerrigan', she cried, 'Poor Kerrigan'.

Her face distorted in pain and grief, she grabbed the hapless Sean by the shoulders and began shaking him. He could see the tears welling up in her eyes just as they welled up in his, and all he could think of was the image of Christ on the cross at Calvary. Later it transpired that the cocky cocker spaniel had somehow lost her footing on top of the wall and had plunged down into the waiting jaws of Sandy, whose patience had been rewarded.

'The services of a vet will not be required', said Sean's father reverently to a distraught Mrs Stevenson who had just witnessed Sandy dragging the dead and battered dog into the open shed.
'Oh the Deadwood stage, came a rolling up over the hill,
Whip crack away, whip crack away, whip crack away'
Sang the wonderful Calamity Jane.

The air around the young teenager darkened and filled with whistling stones which ricocheted off the red brick walls and corrugated tin roof of the lower byre. When the bombardment stopped a great silence filled everywhere as if wads of cotton wool had been stuffed into every crevice and crack in the world. The boy was bemused and felt as if he was cocooned inside the membrane of a pork sausage. Fresian cattle stopped bellowing and no longer dropped their steaming clap with a skittering slap on the cement floor of the byre. Towards evening the cows meandered up the hilly incline from the green of Major Dickson's field, beside the mineral water works to the tarry milking stalls. As the rubber nozzles of the milking machines clasped in a rude handshape the tender tits of their full udders they shuddered with relief and pleasure.

Sean watched his father pasteurising the milk in the asbestos roofed dairy by heating it and then cooling it quickly by letting it flow down over a corrugated aluminium sheet into scalded

Above the Clouds

eight gallon churns. He liked working with his father then, filling the half pint, pint and quart bottles with creamy milk and placing cardboard caps on them. John Jackson, whose brother Aidan had a cleft palate worked about the place and he would tell young Sean wild stories about the shenanigans of his neighbours. He lived in a house in Sloan Street which had an earthen floor, and he delighted Sean by bending a six inch nail with his bare hands and vaulting over a pile of crates in his wellington boots. The wire crates held twenty glass bottles with the words 'Parkview Dairy' printed in a plumb colour on their sides, and when the cream had settled in the narrow neck the cardboard tops were pressed on with the thumb. Each top had the name of the dairy on it along with the words 'grade B' milk. The crates were then stacked in a corner of the dairy and the complete floor was hosed down and swept ready for the morning.

A faded newspaper cutting hung from a nail high up on the wall above the door. Its yellowed paper had curled and twisted around the nail, but the photograph in the centre was still plainly visible. There stood the majestic figure of Joe Louis, and below it the words, 'Heavyweight Champion of the World 1937-1949'. Sean's father admired the Brown Bomber and sometimes he would drop into a crouch and poke out his left hand in imitation of the great boxer. The father would circle around the boy pushing at him and moving to the right, like Joe used to do. 'Hold the centre of the ring' he would say, 'then snap out two left hands before crossing with the right, and boom, right on the chin'.

Young Stribling, the Georgia peach, was another fighter he liked. People had told him that he looked a bit like him, and the fact that a curl of black hair hung down over his right eyebrow just like Stribling's did, amused him. At times like this Sean felt close to his father, and listened to his stories, and the sound of his voice, and the swell and ebb of the words. The gathering together of sounds into spoken lengths that coiled into meandering links of sentences excited him, and in the caverns of his head their cadences swirled around and drifted like leaves in autumn into great eddies. Old words like thee or thou, foreign place names like Marrakesh or Nyasaland, Irish words like gopen or cairn, exotic words like chaos or chic all held his attention. The sounds of these words formed themselves into little rivulets of shapes, line after wavy line until they gushed into a great river of understanding.

Sean's father would often recite exerts from the biblical story of the prodigal son, "And when he was afar off his father seeing him called his servants and said, 'kill ye the fatted calf and prepare a great banquet for my son who was lost but has been found'."
The apparent injustice of the parable both amused and mystified him in equal measure, though not the brutal irony of Shylock in The Merchant of Venice. Because of the unexpected death in the market yard of the boy's grandfather, his own father was taken from boarding school in Newry, and his formal education came to an abrupt end, but not before he had memorised chunks from The Merchant of Venice and Macbeth.

Pulling up the collar of his coat, he would spin around in the dairy, point a long crooked finger at his son, and say,

Above the Clouds

"You call me misbeliever, cut throat dog
And spit upon my Jewish gaberdine,
Should I not say, 'Hath a dog money?'
Is it possible, a cur can lend three thousand ducats?"
Or, he would lean heavily against the kitchen table, and with a melancholy voice say,

"Tomorrow, and tomorrow, and tomorrow,
Creeps in this petty pace from day to day,
To the last syllable of recorded time;
And all our yesterdays have lighted fools
The way to dusty death."

Below the dairy stood the red hay shed with its curved corrugated tin roof. At either end sliding doors hung down from wheels fitted to metal tracks like an upside down railway carriage. It was Sean's job to close over the door nearest the dairy in the evenings but as the wheels were never greased it was far from easy. A small hinged door had been cut into the main door on the left side next to Stevenson's wall. Both doors were secured by a heavy link cow chain which ran through the handles and was fastened with a Yale lock and key. In times past the shed had been filled with loose hay, bags of meal, boxes of apples, heaps of potatoes, piles of sawn and chopped timber, milk churns, horse harness and a scattering of farming tools. Now the interior was a dark empty cave save for tiny beams of light which shone through rusty holes in the tin, criss-crossing the gloom before fraying and fading on the earthy floor. In the cool of the night the candle light shivered, and an epic darkness crept up and over the walls of Troy.

On the day after the twins fourteenth birthday, workmen in blue overalls arrived at the dairy, ripped out the pasteurisation plant and set about converting it into a refrigerated store-room. A large hole was broken in the side wall and a heavy thick door like that in the security vault of a bank was installed. Windows were blocked up and the inside of the store-room was lined with aluminium sheeting. As the ground sloped steeply below the vaulted door a level platform was built with concrete blocks and then smoothed with cement to a glossy hard sheen. This was progress and now the milk could be delivered to Park View depot from the Killyman Co-operative Dairy Society some four miles away. Soon the boys saw plastic crates holding silver-topped bottles of creamy milk being unloaded on to the platform and slid into the cold store every evening where they remained undisturbed until five o'clock the following morning.

Sean, like the medicine men and young braves of the Sioux who gathered at the great camp-fire of their ancestors, dressed in their war bonnets of painted eagle feathers, had begun a slow dance. But their tongues had been cut out and like a silent movie their war chants and whooping could only be imagined. Bright sparks flew up into the night sky from crackling twigs and as they cascaded back to earth their tiny star-like lights lit up the tear stained faces of the painted warriors. Not for them the exhortations of Bunyan's Mr Valiant-for-Truth;

Above the Clouds

"My sword I give to him that shall succeed me in my pilgrimage, and my courage and skill, to him that can get it … So he passed over, and the Trumpets sounded for him on the other side."

The new cold store allowed Sean's father to devote more of his time to his greyhounds. One such dog was called War Chant out of a bitch called Mad Tannis. Pups must be registered with the greyhound Racing Board before they are six months old, and finding a good name for them occupied much of that time. Townlands and local place names were always popular with the doggie men – names like Coolhill Nigger, Lough Neagh Queen or Annaghmore Legend but parochial place names were not for him, instead he would use names from Western movies, like Broken Lance, Silent Arrow, Drifted In and King Colt.

The town boasted two picture houses, and Sean's home, positioned as it was almost midway between the two of them, allowed the family to benefit from their flickering nightly adventures, including Western films. In the square stood the aptly named Castle cinema with its fake turrets and a few hundred yards away in Georges Street was the more flamboyant Astor cinema with its Art Deco pink stucco, tiled steps, chrome railings, coloured strip lighting and glass framed posters. Both picture palaces were owned by a heavy set Jew called Mr Logan, who smoked a fat cigar and owned a cream coloured Bentley car.

Both interior side walls of the Astor had been decorated with panoramic Western murals by a travelling artist called Larry Hayden. Red sandstone bluffs defined an arid dusty plain scattered with gigantic cacti, grey boulders and forlorn pine trees. Above the horizon fluffy clouds smudged with circling black buzzards floated on a pale blue sky. Indian lances, arrows, tomahawks, shields of buffalo hide, and several totem poles were painted rather willy nilly over this vista. Absent from this landscape were herds of shaggy bison, wild eyed horses with blond manes, and thousands of bellowing long horned cattle for they could be seen instead in the real action taking place on the giant moving screen. Millions of years ago the artist's ancestors, deep in the caves of Altamira, depicted the desperate struggles of human survival where the ferocious buffalo thundered through the eternal darkness pursued by naked men with flinty spears and sticks of fire. Now coloured wall lights, shining from Aztec-shaped perspex illuminated a different illusion. Sean, the young Indian, was a regular visitor and grew to love the romance and adventure it offered.

The greyhounds having displaced the livestock were housed in a single storey shed with a sloping roof of asbestos slates. The building was originally used to repair farm machinery and old spades, sythes and hay forks still gathered dust in the corners. At the side of the shed a little gate opened into an old orchard of gnarled apple trees and spikey gooseberry bushes. Beyond the orchard a small sloping field divided by a pot-holed path led down to an iron gated laneway. The homestead petered out at the gate, and the songs of many birds could be heard calling from the green hedgerows and white blossomed thorn trees along the twist of the pollen-filled lane.

About midday, John the milk vendor would return from the grind of ordinariness. Up the yard to the house he would march armed with the Irish News, his milk book and a couple of

Above the Clouds

large brown loaves, whose shiny domes glistened like varnish on a dining-room table. In the back kitchen the fresh, plump coarse-grained bread was hacked into jagged sections with a butcher's knife by Sean, the dog handling apprentice. The bread was then spread around two deep sided tin trays, which bore the embossed stamp 'Wherry's Hotel' on their sides. Sean would nibble at this delicious bread when unobserved and sometimes he would even secret bits of it in his trouser pockets for later, for he much preferred it to milled white bread, like the White Chief pan or the square batch loaf with its black crusty dome, which his mother bought.

Five or six large hair-cracked eggs were broken over the bread on each tray and these eggs bought in cardboard trays from Carson's egg-store on the Newell Road, often had double yokes. Then Sean poured warm milky tea, from a large black assed teapot over the mixture. The boy and the man carried the steaming food trays down the yard past the red shed to the sound of the howling and yelping greyhounds. Once a week a sheep's head was boiled in a large black pot on the kitchen fire. Every so often Sean would lift off the lid and manoeuvre the steaming cranium around the boiling pot with a poker.

Then the kitchen filled with the delicious aroma of cooking sheep flesh and brains and Sean envied the sleek thoroughbreds their forthcoming feast. This white meat, like offal and tripe was not for human consumption, warned his mother, but Sandy enjoyed chewing on the bones of the blanched skull.

The boys, now frisky and awkward came in for some special attention from their mother who decided to dress them in identical outfits. Their humiliation was complete when they were kitted out in two of everything bought in Donaghue's drapery shop in Irish Street. They wore pale grey short trousers with snake belts, knee length dark grey socks held up with knicker elastic, brown leather sandals with enormous side buckles, cream short-sleeved shirts, and the uniform was completed with a sleeveless pullover decorated with a zig-zag pattern down the front.

'Oh, it's the twins', complete strangers would exclaim when they were paraded like prize exhibits at the annual Clogher Valley agriculture show, and Joe McDoakes peeped out from behind the eight ball.

There were three sets of twins around the same age living in Scotch Street, and they all dwelt just a few doors apart. Above Stevenson's house, at number fifty lived the McConkey girls, Sheila and Margaret, whose father Jerry was an ebullient and energetic doctor distinguished by pinched features, rosy cheeks and darting close-set eyes. He always sported a tweed jacket enlivened with a red floppy silk handkerchief which hung down from the breast pocket, and it was said that he inherited a lot of money from an old uncle who had died in America. During the summer months the girls often played with Sean's sister Eileen, some ten months younger, when they were paroled from boarding school.

Their hair platted in a loose careless fashion was rather at odds with their quiet determined demeanour. This was in marked contrast to the Hamill twin girls who lived directly opposite

Above the Clouds

them in a pebble-dashed house which belonged to the Presbyterian church. Mary and Elizabeth were tall and gregarious with masses of curly black hair, flashing eyes and flailing arms, and their father Wallace owned a grocery shop and meal store.

All the twins played regularly in the store among the heavy jute bags, their tied tops sitting up like the ears of a jack donkey. Sammy, a baldy sturdy man from Milltown, filled smaller bags with yellow meal into which he mixed brown nuts, shaped like clove rock, which he claimed the cattle loved. Then he would sew the bags at the top with hemp string and stencil numbers on the side with a black brush. On the twelfth of July every year Sammy exchanged his dungarees for a black suit, white shirt, bowler hat and orange sash. As he marched proudly down Scotch Street from the Lord Northland memorial hall, resplendent in his regalia, the boys would wave shyly as he passed their house.

About five o'clock in the morning Sean would awaken to the familiar sounds of his father moving about in the bedroom next to his. He waited for the creaking sound of his footsteps on the floorboards outside his door, the rap rap of his knuckles and the voice saying, 'are you up?'. 'Right', came the reply.

His father was never one for saying a lot, even when he had a few drinks in him, but for Sean the sound of his echoing voice around and about the empty husky kernel of the house filled the air. To the boy the daily milk round, even in summer was just a chore of endless bottles left on doorsteps, empties collected and crates stacked enlivened only by desultory banter and idle gossip.

'Look at the state of those empties', his father would declare, 'That Mrs O'Neill is a right lazy bitch. Those youngsters will have to rear themselves.' Washed returns on the other hand were a sure sign of a disciplined household.

In the winter months however things were more difficult, for the dark seemingly eternal chill turned the town into a brooding secretive place in the hours before daylight. Like Scott of the Antarctic energies had to be conserved in the biting cold, there was little talk and Sean moved with the efficiency and purpose of a seal under the polar ice-cap. Frosty mornings could be handled but constant rain or incessant mizzle crept in under jackets and caps and even skin itself until bone and sinew began to dissolve into a mouldy mulch. The warm cab of the Bedford lorry, where the engine was encased between the seats provided some relief and a little comfort.

Except for holiday times Sean only helped out at the weekends, but he became aware of his father's endless excursion to nowhere. From the coldstore he circumnavigated the globe of the town but unlike Magellan his voyages were predictable and pointless, and his guiding stars were the towns sinewy streets and the new peripheral housing estates. Down short highway into Milltown and past Dickson's factory, where during the war parachutes for airmen and wing coverings for the mosquito fighter planes of the airforce had been made, he sailed. Then up the sweeping Ranfurly Road and around Cunninghams Lane, the south-westerly winds carried him. With full sail the milk captain glided around by the chapel, the Circular Road, the White City and the Oaks Road. Westward in a freshening breeze he reached the new hospital, the

Above the Clouds

Drumcoo Estate, and onwards into Irish Street, Ann Street and the safety of the town square. A gusty freshening wind carried him east towards the Quarry Lane, the Donaghmore Road, and the Newell Road. The spice islands of Beechvalley were now in sight and the familiar skyline of Victoria Road came into view. Sailing into the wide safe harbour of Parkview Bay he would drop anchor as the ship's bell tolled twelve. Unloading bales of cotton from deep in the hold the old sea captain began singing snatches from 'The Man from Laramie'.

"He was a man with so many notches on his gun, that ..... the arguing or fighting, fighting was this man's speciality ..... the man from Laramie...."

As he was finishing his tea Sean heard the slam of the yard gate and a few seconds later the grinning face of Herbie Johnston appeared at the kitchen window. Herbie and Sean's father were friends of a sort, and he would often regale the boys with stories of his exploits with the Enniskilling Fusiliers during the second world war, but nothing about his later membership of the 'B' special police force. By day he was the superintendent of the market yard and kept an eye on the place for the rate payers of the town. They were strange bedfellows but shared an abiding interest in birds and animals.

The two men, followed by the curious boy walked down past the cold store, through the red shed and into the old orchard to a place where a shallow hole had been dug. A spade stuck out of a pile of grassy sods and loose soil and stones. The dairyman turned to the boy, saying, "Take one of the leads and bring me down Sands."

Sands of Dee, to give the greyhound its full name was a big golden animal who had committed the cardinal sin of showing no interest in savaging smaller animals to death. Somehow the killer instinct of the species was absent, and as a consequence the fate of the dog was sealed for he may as well have been an elephant without a trunk. When the young dogs are about eight months old they take part in a series of trials to assess their racing potential. A few days earlier a trial had been arranged at the town's Oaks Park dog track, and when the electric hare sped past the traps poor Sands just ambled out showing no interest in the fast disappearing furry motor.

The dog lover took the lead from Sean and patting Sands gently he stood the fawn dog in the earthy hole. Herbie had remained motionless all this time with his hands deep in his jacket pockets. He was a heavy man with glasses perched on wide nostrils, above which a shock of white hair crowned his ample head. His right hand came out of his pocket holding a cocked revolver, and he just shot Sands between the eyes.

The dog crumpled and went down like a court marshalled soldier in a Flanders poppy field. The gunman looked with wry amusement at the shocked expression on Sean's face before putting the gun back in his pocket, and handing him the spade. The adults retreated and the boy was left to conceal the conspiracy. In Hungary the Russian tanks rolled into Budapest.

The man never spoke to the boy about the death of the dog. Once a year, on the Sunday before the anniversary of his grandfather's demise the two of them would visit the Carland Road

Above the Clouds

cemetery, his father to familiarise himself yet again with its granite configuration. Sean liked wandering around and tracing his fingers along the cold incised letters and numerals inscribed on the headstones. ... in loving memory of .... Sacred heart of Jesus ... who departed this world ... on 4th February 1943. James Quinn ... Oliver Cullen ... John Keenan ... Requescant in Pace.

Behind the boundary wall the ground slopes gently towards the distant foothills of the Sperrins, and under their feet the heavy blue clay is speckled with wet bones. Carved and decorated crosses with shafts defining the skyline are slotted in between more modest granite or marble memorials. Sean stopped at the family memorial near the centre of the graveyard, its eight foot high celtic cross etched with the names of forebearers he never knew. There they lie, he mused, three abreast, waiting under a coating of marble chips, in this annex to heaven. Godot's waiting room, where only the haunted, the homeless, the displaced, and the sentimental ever visited.

"Hail Queen of heaven, star of the sea,
Pray for the wanderer, pray for me
Save us from peril, save us from woe,"

Sean would sing during October devotions in the dreary gothic splendour of Saint Patrick's church.

For the teenage boy the sight of his thirty eight year old father making himself at home among the dead was unsettling, and hanging about a cemetery for very long was not his idea of fun. This was a boothill for worn out cowboys, faded saloon girls and crazy gunslingers, and not a repository for the fit and able. Just then a shower of hailstones descended from the darkened sky overhead and they fled the place.

Sean's father never talked much about his family and for the boy's part he never thought much about them either, after all he had his own life to lead. Occasional visits by uncles and aunts did however put faces to the names of his relations. His uncle Seamus, who lived in Belfast, had a small round face with intense blue eyes while his aunt Eileen by contrast had an angular bony face complete with a strangulated accent honed by living for years in London. Behind the certainty of their names their lives were as real to him as the elongated shadows of strangers that criss-crossed the streets of the town.

His family now eight in number had supplanted in the house all those of an earlier generation who had just gone away and disappeared. The last person to be displaced was his granny who had retreated to several rooms sandwiched between the ground floor living rooms and the bedrooms on the third floor. The relationship between her and Sean's mother was an uneasy one, but for reasons unknown she just left and went to live with his aunt Ann in Belfast, and the vacated rooms were rented out to the electricity board.

Above the Clouds

The livestock who had once filled the yards, outhouses and sheds were also all gone though their presence clung for a while in the air like a bed that had recently been slept in. The empty buildings, now functionally redundant, began to turn in on themselves. At first they seemed quietly relieved but Sean noticed that they began to murmur among themselves at the loss of the animals and their human handlers.

They seemed to resent the absence of shouting and yelling yards-men coupled with the snorting and bellowing of excited cattle and pigs. The boy sensed that the place was growing cold and even morose, and at night he occasionally heard the stones and timbers crying and howling with the wind. Sometimes their fury enveloped the entire house, and windows rattled, doors slammed and slates flung from the roof were dashed to pieces in the yard below. In the mornings after a stormy night they remained sodden and sullen with water cascading over blocked gutters and lying like swollen pools of mercury on the cracked concrete below.

The greyhounds who now occupied a few sheds were hardly adequate companions for the beleaguered out-buildings surrounded by those tall high boundary walls, which in reality provided little protection. Betrayal and dishonour awaited them like the Indians of the great plains who watched with dismay the arrival of the pale faces in their lumbering wagons. Like leaves in autumn they would soon sweep over the land in search of the yellow stone, and the pony soldiers in their uniforms of navy and yellow would spit death from their fire sticks.

Sean watched with some discontent as his home and the buildings around it became increasingly dysfunctional. Soon even the adjoining fields with their laden hedges and swaying trees began to look unkempt and uncared for. Long wavy grasses appeared everywhere, young willowy branches prodded the air and spiky thorn bushes by the far lane glistened and beckoned to unsuspecting butterflies. The old pear tree whose twisted branches leaned heavily against the dairy wall refused to bear fruit as if in protest against the neglect all around it.

The house itself suffered the paralysis of uncertainty, as window frames warped and became impossible to slide up or down, and wilfully resisted brute force, candle wax or the splintering attention of a screw driver. Flower pots filled with scarlet geraniums dislodged themselves from the kitchen window ledge and died where they fell, and shards of red clay lay on the flagstones waiting to be embedded in the soft flesh of baby hands. Rivulets of black tar crept unnoticed down the sides of drain pipes and spread into the helpless gullies as storm clouds of deep purple rumbled and crashed and filled the sky above the house with the roar of rolling thunder.

In the Astor cinema bombardier Billy Wells ex-heavyweight champion of Britain smote the gong for J. Arthur Rank seconds before the start of another silvery movie.

Above the Clouds

2

By the age of nineteen Sean was a dreamy student at a teacher training college in Belfast with his head full of Satre and Hemingway. He believed most things he read, including the words, "man is not made for defeat, a man can be destroyed but he cannot be defeated", wrote his hero Hemingway in the novella "The Old Man and the Sea". In fact he saw himself as a kind of latter-day guru whose vocation in life was to dispense advice to broken-hearted lovers and star-crossed adolescents. He was heading straight for the rebel without a cause syndrome.

Since going to college that September his normal practice was to hitch a lift on a Friday afternoon to his home in Gannon's hilly fortress by journeying the forty miles or so through the marshy acres which spread themselves out like a soggy quilt west of the river Bann. This meant skipping a boring lecture on child psychology from a grey haired man in suede shoes. Sean and another like-minded individual called 'Gunner' Hagan from Armagh would walk down from the 'ranch' as it was known, to Finaghy crossroads at the junction of which stood the Tivoli cinema. They needed to be on the road by about three o'clock before the student nurses arrived, for naturally enough the vehicles always stopped for them first. There was no point in even sticking out your thumb to a passing lorry if a couple of girls in hipster jeans looked vaguely in the direction of the lone male driver.

On this particular Friday only Sean (for Gunner had fallen in love with a girl who lived in Andersonstown) positioned himself opposite the fake stone façade of the Free Presbyterian church and made energetic thumb movements at the oncoming traffic.

He waited for about twenty minutes before a white Ford van with the name 'Olivetti Typewriters' painted in black letters on its side pulled up. In the follow up conversation it emerged that the driver, called Jack Ferguson was a greyhound follower and knew Sean's dad.

'Has he entered anything for the McAlevey?' he queried as they drove along the main street of Dunmurry village and out towards Derriaghey. The McAlevey gold cup was awarded annually to the winner of a premier hare coursing event held at Crebilly near Ballymena, and as it happened his father had a good brindle bitch called Brazilian Beat that was entered for the cup. A few weeks earlier they had blooded the bitch along with its half-brother called 'Fields Afar', up in O'Brien's hilly field which ran parallel to the Black Lough or Baile na Saggart as the Gaelic leaguers called it. Sean's father now owned a blue Bedford flat-backed truck for delivering the milk, though he never got round to having the words 'Parkview Dairy' painted on the vehicle, probably surmising that everyone knew who he was anyway.

Above the Clouds

Sean crouched down on the back of the truck holding two excited dogs by their leads as his father drove up Beechvalley and around Windmill Hill to the upturned saucer of the field. A wide swinging gate with the letter R for Ranfurly welded on to the diagonal bars was pushed open and a man with a lumpy meal sack and a younger man holding two yelping hounds made their way to the corner of the pasture. Then the young man stopped and watched as his father continued walking for about a hundred yards until his diminutive outline was silhouetted against the majesty of a blue sky like a Galway turf-cutter in a Paul Henry landscape. Sean stood motionless between the straining glassy-eyed animals, keeping his eyes focused on the figure at the brow of the hill. With the ends of the leads tied together he held a dog collar in each hand with the metal pins turned back so that they would slip easily away from the dogs' necks. They sensed the moment, standing stock still, rigid yet poised like coiled springs.

It seemed a long time before the man now the size of a midget stopped walking, then turning he raised a white handkerchief above his head and began waving it. Sean jerked the collars free and the dogs hurtled towards the far horizon as the figure bent down and leisurely loosened the top of the sack which was now laying in tufty grass at his feet. A bewildered hare burst out pausing for a split second, on seeing the howling dogs dashing towards it, before bounding towards a distant white thorn hedge. But a long line of twine tied around its chest somersaulted the hare to a shocked halt in a couple of seconds, for the other end of the twin was looped around the doggie man's wrist. The dogs were nearly on it before the petrified animal dashed towards their teeth in a suicidal act of crazy bravery. As the dogs tore it apart its strangulated baby-like cries filled the air, and a couple of fresian cattle disturbed by the noise looked up for a second, their jaws still chewing the cud, before dipping their heads again into the green sward.

'Tomorrow the black birds would come', wrote Satre at the conclusion of his trilogy, 'Iron in the Soul'.

Sean's new acquaintance, Jack the Olivetti salesman, dropped him off right at his front door, the number of which had changed for reasons unknown to him from Stevie Bloomfield's black enamel fifty four to Johnny McGirr's brass thirty eight. A spectacular autumn sunset bathed the door in an odd peppermint coloured effervescent glow, and pushing it open it felt like a giant marshmallow. He thought of the witches in Hansel and Gretel whose house was built of bread and roofed with cakes, and the windows were made of transparent honey.

The long hall leading to the sitting room was awash with colour – dabs of red, dashes of yellow, streaks of blue, trails of yellow, splashes of purple and splatters of white covered the entire walls, ceiling, floor and stairs in a glorious tribute to Jackson Pollock. Abstract expressionism had crossed the Atlantic and lay hidden and undisturbed in provincial Ulster.

From the window in his bedroom he could see that the fields once green had turned to purple and gold in the mothy evening light, and the brick facades of the new houses down the Carland

Above the Clouds

Road glowed a delicate pink. He felt sure that the blood in his veins if tapped would run like the swirling candy colour stripes around the pole outside Joe Finnegan's barber shop in Irish Street.

In the brightness of the morning the air itself was filled with wondrous sounds and rhythms of a new music which seemed to have crept almost unnoticed from under doors, carpets and even the stones on the road to explode in the sky above the town like cartwheels and Roman candles at Halloween.

'Heavenly shades of night are falling, its twilight time out of the mist your voice is calling, its twilight time' sang the wonderful Platters.

'Oh ah, oh ah,' warbled the swaying backing group of three black men in shining tuxedoes and a beautiful black girl in a pale blue strapless evening gown covered in millions of glittering sequins.

The young nineteen year old buck was ready to take on the world.

He began to spend Saturday afternoons in the Ranfurly café, the grooviest joint in town. Red formica covered tables some with wobbly legs were scattered around a first-floor room which boasted two large sash windows. The tables near the windows were always at a premium as the lucky patrons could survey the goings on of the town's inhabitants from this elevated vantage point. The building had originally been a hotel and the impressive coat of arms of the Ranfurly family, whose ancestors had dominated the politics of the area for several centuries, was sculpted in high relief on the wall between the windows. The Georgian façade has been given a lick of paint with bright colours and the coat of arms had been carelessly touched-up giving the entire building an unintentional air of theatricality, even farce. Stevie Bloomfield, drunk or sober, would never have been guilty of such pictorial sloppiness. Even the Athenian warriors, plunging horses and vestial virgins sculpted by Pheidias in the pediments of the Acropolis in ancient Greece would have been expertly and meticulously painted by Stevie.

The focal point of the café was the futuristic chrome juke-box which consumed an endless meal of three penny bits and sixpences, and in return belted out a fantastic selection of American pop music. "Be my baby", by the raunchy Ronettes, "Why do fools fall in love", sang the energetic Frankie Limon and The Teenagers, "Hats off to Larry", warbled Del Shannon, "Oh, Carol", crooned Neil Sadaka, Elvis mumbled and strummed his way through "Loving You", and Sean's favourite song of all, the Texacana ballad "Only the Lonely", sang by the incomparable Roy Orbison.

This was the music of love and the inevitable pain that accompanies it. The scent of cheap perfume was everywhere, and mingled with cigarette smoke and the aroma of coffee it formed a delicious opiate which invigorated those lonely souls who wandered languidly in and out of the café like extras in a William Hopper painting.

Big Roach Loughran, Liam 'Hannibal' Hamill, Paul 'Dino' Dean, his cousin Harry Hughes, Alec Donnelly and Sean would hang out together, either in the café or more often in the entrance hallway. To reach the café the patrons had to run the gauntlet of this milling group,

Above the Clouds

who stood around for most of the afternoon talking about girls, music, girls, films, girls, cars, and more girls. Occasionally the owner of the café, Mrs Wherry, a big woman in a black dress would descent the stairs and tell the dudes to 'clear off' as her customers had complained of being jostled and laughed at. She lived in a fine detached house faced with cut stone near Victoria Road, where some years earlier a lodger had been convicted of the murder of a local girl who was pregnant by him. The story had made the English Sunday newspapers and the case involved detectives from Scotland Yard coming over to help solve the murder.

Her complaints however fell on deaf ears for the gang were only interested in chatting up any girls who passed by and many of them welcomed their attentions. Their derogatory comments were reserved for a variety of innocent pedestrians going about their business in the square. "Christ, look at the size of your woman's tits", Roach would say to loud guffaghs. "Where in God's name did O'Neill get those crazy trousers?", Sean would cry to more guffaghs. "My God she's got an ass like the back of a UTA bus", Alec would roar, pointing in the direction of an unfortunate shop assistant crossing the road.

"Hi Tom, who lent you the Queen's scarf?", Harry would shout at a first year university student who made the mistake of parading his scarf like an intellectual badge of merit. The lads themselves were of course perfect specimens of Irish manhood.

Tom O'Rourke, the Queen's University fresher was an only child who lived in a house near the top of a steep hill. From where the boys stood they could see the road which ran up past a row of Kafkaesque like dwellings as far as the crumbling towers of O'Neill's castle on the summit. From its battlemented top could be seen all the six counties, that is if one was allowed into the grounds, but as it was occupied by the Territorial Army, no-one could go there.

These houses were only kept from tumbling down the hill by a set of three-storey late Georgian tenements with ground level shops, which were built into the corner of the town square. Traders and their families, such as the Stewarts, the Cahoons, and the Alexanders lived and loved over these premises.

In the centre of the square itself stood the loneliest man in the world. This soldier of the great war who, being cast in bronze, allowed his helmet, uniform and rifle to be soiled with bird shit. He never flinched, however, up there on his pedestal of stone, and leaning on his rifle he gazed southwards and just waited. Sometimes the sun shone full on his face and sometimes the wind howled around his head, but it never bothered this warrior of war. His triumph was his folly and he just stood there, homo erectus, forlorn, exhausted and exalted.

The boxed outline of the square perched as it was on the side of Drumglass drumlin could be an unforgiving kind of place, especially during the autumn and winter months. The sad, earnest men who preached there on Saturday nights would have you believe that the town was a place of idolatry and drunkenness.

Above the Clouds

"Repent now, ye sinners, and you will be saved. Only by being born again can you inherit the kingdom of God" they roared with Ballymena accents through grey megaphones. Sean marvelled at their persistence and at their ability to quote chunks of the bible from memory, and sometimes their personal statements were genuinely moving. Occasionally they would be joined by their women folk, and when a good looking young woman stood in their midst the lads listened attentively and lingered just long enough to catch her eye.

In the winter months rain, sleet and snow swirled and roared around the sloping quadrangle, pelting the Ionic pilasters of the Ulster Bank and whistling around the gable end of McAleer's Hotel. Neither of these buildings, their history or appearance or any of the town's buildings were of little interest to 'the dudes', as they had begun to call themselves. Architects like William Henry Lynn whose Belfast Bank boasted barley-sugar corner insets, or James H Owens' stone police fortress with its Scotch baronial crow-stepped gables did their best to give the town an air of respectability, but the only buildings which interested the dudes were those that allowed them to come into close contact with members of the opposite sex. Hence restaurants, chip shops, cafes, dance halls and picture houses became their modus operandi.

Next door to the Ranfurly café was Dickies' restaurant, where the prim mothers of girls which the lads lusted after drank tea and nibbled on squares of shortbread covered with chocolate. A few doors further down on the corner of Church Street was situated Miss Burton's sweet shop and ice-cream parlour. Older people, strangers from outside the town sat at round tables scooping ice-cream from out of glass dessert bowls with long silvery spoons, their parcels, hats and handbags piled on vacant cane chairs.

Such places were not normally frequented by the dudes unless of course a nice looking girl worked there. Then chocolate, sweets and cigarettes were bought in a vain attempt to chat her up.

"Give us a quarter of liquorice allsorts", Sean would drawl, his eyes devouring the body under the shop coat, and in the same breath would add, "You were looking well the other night"
"Why, am I not looking well now?", Rose, Miss Burton's black haired assistant cheekily answered, as she swept the sweets off the scales and into a white paper bag. It was always a good sign if she deliberately weighed out more than the four ounces, but on this occasion, Rose, if anything gave Sean a couple of allsorts less than he was entitled to. Undeterred he said,
"You always look well right enough", and handing her a shilling said, "Was that your boyfriend you were with?" "It might have been", came the dismissive reply from the ice maiden, followed by, "and is there anything else you would like?".

3

On a warm Saturday afternoon the young man saw her in a painted canvas under a Van Gogh sun, a happy girl in a spotted cotton dress and sun cream in her bag. 'How beautiful she is', he thought. For what seemed an eternity he observed her move towards him in the street of dreams, her long sinewy shadow finally embracing and then engulfing him as they drew nearer. A voice inside him said, 'speak to her quickly before she passes by'.

"Isn't it a lovely day", he croaked and as the words fell from his parched mouth he loved her with a passion known only to the gods. She laughed at the sound of his voice and her teeth were very white. He wondered why he had never noticed her before and in the swirling brushstrokes of the sky above them, black painted birds were buffeted by blue and grey winds.
"It's very warm", she replied, and looking directly into his eyes of blue said, "and my name is Eleanor".

Then she was gone, her dress dancing in the light but like Lot's wife he was afraid to turn around and gaze after her, but he knew that he was happier than the had ever been before.
"Why didn't I stop and chat her up a bit?", he asked himself reproachfully, and in his head he could hear Roy Orbison singing "Dream baby, dream baby, how long must I dream?". Beneath him the pavement wobbled and then her voice, hundreds of voices, all belonging to her, repeated in chorus the name Eleanor, over and over, and over.

"I've lost her now", he moaned to himself in the depths of his love and distress. He wanted to run away, to run down the hill and up the dizzy stairs of his home and hide his head under the pillows in his bedroom, and lie there all night tossing and trembling in the bed with her laughing voice resonating in his brain. But though the moment my be lost, he reasoned, he was damned if he would run from his first proper love to lie sobbing and sniffling into a pillow of damp feathers. The dazed young man saw the outline of the town through a misty haze and he trembled for a girl with a sunshine smile and apple blossom in her hair had just entered his life. Unknown to him William Butler Yeats had already seen her years before and had drawn her into a wondrous poem.

"What's up with you", queried Sean's pals as they sat in Pagni's chip shop-cum- restaurant located at the far corner of the square next to Fred W Robinson's hardware emporium. He told them of the beautiful girl he had seen, and having ordered four bottles of coca-cola and a single chip with four forks, these young men of destiny plotted how to capture the heart of a long-legged shop assistant.

Dino who lived up Irish Street was considered a bit of a lad inside the rambling confines of the town's narrow streets. He was, after all wise in the ways of women, for being a projectionist in the Astor cinema he had studied hundreds of celluloid reels of film where romantic encounters between the species was the main ingredient.

The plan was a simple one. Dino would approach the beautiful Eleanor during her lunch hour and engage her in conversation, politely enquiring if she knew Sean, and in effect chat her up on his behalf. If she was free the following Saturday night, it was suggested, Sean would like to take her to the pictures. The plan of course was far from foolproof, for it occurred to Sean that Dino, whose silky words rolled off his tongue like warm butter dripping off toast, might decide to date her himself and risk incurring the terrible wrath of his friends.

On the other hand the onus was on Eleanor to come into town on the bus, for she lived in the nearby housing estate called the 'White City', to meet Sean, who after all was a townie. In a manner of speaking the mountain must come to Mohammed.

The following Friday afternoon Jack the Olivetti salesman spied the pensive Sean standing on the footpaths edge at Finaghy crossroads. The van stopped and a grateful Sean thrust himself through the passenger door.

"Good looking birds", said Jack pointing in the direction of two girls with thumbs outstretched, who were standing some twenty yards away.
"Maybe we could squeeze them in", he continued. But Sean, now comfortably ensconced beside him, and with his duffle bag between his knees churlishly replied, "They're a couple of stuck-up cows out of the Royal, I wouldn't touch them with a barge pole."
Surprised at the remark Jack accelerated westwards up the hill and headed towards Lisburn town.

"Do you want a cigarette?", asked Jack, taking a packet of ten Gallagher Blues from his pocket.
"No thanks", came the reply.

"You're in great form with yourself", said Jack lighting a cigarette and throwing the spent match out of the window. Deliberately blowing smoke in Sean's direction he went on, "judging by your face that college of yours must be a sad sort of a place".

For Sean the teacher training college was a bit of a disappointment alright, as the place seemed full of freaks, half-wits, gamblers and worst of all educational zealots. In his mind he felt a bit guilty for being less than sociable to Jack who, after all was giving him a ride home and anyway it was an unwritten rule among the thumbing fraternity that the onus was on them to make conversation in exchange for a lift. But the young student had fallen head over heels in

love with a divine goddess and had spent a miserable week wondering if Dino had succeeded in getting him 'fixed up'.
"Earth angel, earth angel, won't you be mine,
My dearest darling, love you all the time',
Sang teenage pop groups at Friday night hops all over American high school campuses.

Sean was also dog tired having lain awake for hours on end tossing and turning in the pitch darkness of his lonely dormitory, and when sleep did come it was a shallow troubled slumber shot through with frightening hallucinations. In his dreams lumps of concrete fell from the sky, crashed through the ceiling above him and landed with a terrific thud on his chest. From the depths of his nightmare he peered up through the gaping hole in the universe and saw a maiden with flowing hair riding on a purple unicorn. When he awoke he was both shocked and exhilarated and never having been bewitched by a girl before, was at a loss to understand his feelings.

"I saw this fabulous girl last Saturday", Sean began, but his beaming face betrayed him and before he could say another word Jack let out a loud guffagh and slapped him roughly on the side of the head.
"Oh, my Christ, you're in love you silly prick", he roared.
"No, I'm not", replied Sean, "I hardly know her".

The van with the painted typewriters transported the two of them along bumpy roads and around a series of huge earthworks where an instant city was being assembled like an enormous stage-set for a play bereft of plot or players. Over the river Bann they swept into Portadown and turning right in the centre of high street they headed ever westwards into orchard county and concrete roads with high hedges over which leaned knarled bramley branches laden with their swollen harvest of apples. Jack continued to probe, "What's this lassie's name, if you don't mind me asking?"
Sean silently repeated the name Eleanor over and over in his mind rolling the three syllables round his tongue like boiled sweets before he heard himself saying,
"For your information, Jack, she's called Eleanor and she works in McManus's sweetshop in Scotch Street. I'm taking her to the pictures tomorrow night, so I am", Sean said hopefully. He tried to sound confident but he wouldn't know till he reached home if Dino had even managed to speak to Eleanor.
"What side of the house is she?" queried Jack.
The question, was totally unexpected.
"I don't know, and I don't care", answered Sean uneasily.
Jack wagged his finger under the nose of the young man, and in a voice that was both reassuring and vaguely threatening said, "Go out with whoever you like, enjoy yourself, but

don't get serious with a girl from a different persuasion or you'll be bringing a pile of trouble down on yourself."

The stony curve of Dargan's bridge over the Blackwater River rose to meet them as they approached the village of Moy and the boundary between counties Armagh and Tyrone. Without a further word Jack stopped the van at the foot of the hill along side Patterson's abandoned stone mill, behind which the weed-choked mid-Ulster canal waited in vain for restoration.

He walked across the street and disappeared through the glass fronted doors of a drapery store above which the words 'Stewart ladies and gents outfitters', were hand painted in neat gold and black lettering. Stevie Bloomfield probably painted it, Sean mused to himself.

He looked at the clothed dummies in the window and thought about his family. Every year on the Twelfth of July morning they would watch from their front door the Orange brethren triumphantly march down the street from the Viceroy hall at Castle Hill.

The parade would complete the circuit of the town by turning left into Barrack Street, down into Milltown and past Dicksons' factory, then up Wellington Road before swinging left along Ranfurly Road and into Perry Street. Finally a stiff climb up Church Street and under the spire of St Anne's Church before the marchers entered the square itself and dispersed around the war memorial. Streets such as William Street, Ann Street, and Irish Street which were largely Nationalist were avoided.

Sean's father often joked that from his vantage point he would take the salute of the passing marchers, many of whom he knew well, and sure enough a few of them would nod shyly in his direction or give a timid white gloved wave. Sammy Abernethy who worked in Hamilton's meal yard, a few shops above them always raised his bowler hat to his mother. The parade was alternatively headed either by the Howard Memorial pipe band or the local silver band, who always played 'The Sash' with great gusto, the words of which were known to everyone.

"It is old but it is beautiful
And its colours they are fine
It is worn at Derry, Aughrim, Enniskillen and the Boyne
My father wore it as a youth
In bye-gone days of yore
And on the twelfth I love to wear
The sash my father wore."

Behind the band the office bearers of the lodge, proud hard hatted men in charcoal grey suits and sashes of orange and silver strode with military precision, some of them with flashing ceremonial swords held at the ready. Then came the swaying silk banner depicting King William at the battle of the Boyne, carried by two straining brethren flanked by junior Orangemen holding the long tassled ropes. The rank and file members some without hats marched behind the banner, their meandering column held in good order under the watchful eyes of the ceremonial lance bearers at the rear.

Once every few years the town was the host venue for all the lodges of South Tyrone and then a large gathering of god-fearing Orangemen, their families and groups of swaggering bandsmen would converge on the flag bedecked streets. Banners from lodges in Newmills, Aughnacloy, Laghey, Edentilone, Ballymacall, Mulnagore, Pomeroy and the Bawn billowed and swelled like the sails of clipper ships at anchor, and told their stories of Moses on the mount, the Ulster divisions at the Somme, the defenders of Londonderry and battle scenes from Aughrim and the Boyne. Red white and blue bunting strung across the streets, criss-crossed the walls, doors and windows of houses with black shadowy furrows.

Thundery Lambeg drums decorated with sprays of orange lilies were flailed by sweating men in their shirt sleeves who walked forward slowly and solemnly, their supporters mesmerised by the relentless rhythm. Other bandsmen filled the streets with the music of their pipes, flutes and accordions, their tunes usually accompanied by the growling menace of many drums.

Only once did the Orange jamboree anger Sean's father. On a particular fine evening before the Twelfth, council workmen were stringing bunting from one side of the street to the other. A man called Syd Wylie had scrambled up a ladder by the door where Sean and his father were standing, and had looped the bunting around the drainpipe of the house. When he climbed down to street level the father said casually, "Syd, you've got the bunting on the wrong drainpipe."

"That's where it goes every year", replied Syd, and started to remove the ladder.
Sean watched his father's face darken as he said, "If you don't take if off my drainpipe it'll be cut off."

The remark flustered Syd who withdrew his hand from the ladder, but the council foreman, an ex-service man who had fought in North Africa during the second world war, stepped forward and said, "If you look up, Syd, you'll see that the bunting should be attached to Mr Stevenson's drainpipe."

The return of Jack to the van ended the student's reverie, and on the way into town they talked about the big fight due to take place in the King's Hall at Balmoral. Both were of the opinion that Freddie Gilroy would get the better of Johnny Caldwell, who had fought two bruising battles against Alphonse Halami and the Brazilian world champion Eder Jofre. It would be a great fight and Sean who had already bought a ticket was looking forward to it. When the young student of pugilism walked in to the kitchen of his home his father looked up from the newspaper and said, "It says here that Gilroy may have trouble making the weight."

Several evenings a week Sean would leave his fellow students watching television in the common-room of their red-bricked college and walk the mile or so until he reached St Theresa's

Above the Clouds

hall on the Falls Road. There he mingled with men and lads whose only interest revolved around boxing, or as A J Leibling called it, 'The Sweet Science".

The noble art, he claimed was a sport joined on to the past like a man's arm to his elbow, and that the best of its practitioners like Joe Louis or Sugar Ray Robinson, light up the firmament in both directions historically, exposing the insignificance of what preceded and followed. The heroes of Boxiana, Sean sensed, stood alone, even Hemingway understood that, and their sweat and aggression was the natural by-product of a distillation process started in the watery Jurassic caves of an embryonic planet. Pierce Egan referred to these men as 'the milling coves', and on Tuesday and Thursday nights they gathered in the gym in pursuit of a common goal.

A few years earlier Sean and his brother had cycled the eleven miles to Armagh to see a film called, 'The Champion'. The picture starred Kirk Douglas as a world title contender and Arthur Kennedy as his brother and manager. On their journey home they cycled past the elegant Georgian buildings of the Mall and out past McCarthy's twin-towered cathedral on the hill.

In the gym as in the film youths pounded the heavy bag, shadow boxed and skipped while inside the roped coliseum the gloved gladiators learned how to feint and move, throw a straight left or a right hook, slip out of range or cover up, dance or use the ropes, land an uppercut or block a right cross. Sometimes Sean would don the heavy gloves and spar a few rounds, but exhaustion soon replaced his enthusiasm, and he would lie in bed at night nursing a sore jaw or bruised ribs and ponder how fistic defeat can be such an honourable thing.

He had seen Hogan 'Kid' Bassey destroy British and Empire featherweight champion Billy 'Spider' Kelly and watched the Belfast southpaw John Kelly being knocked-out by the French-Algerian flyweight Robert Cohen. At a fight in the King's Hall he marvelled at a shouting fan whose ignorance of the ring was exceeded only by his unwillingness to face facts. At the Kelly fight a man near him shouted, "He can't hurt you, John. He can't hurt nobody!", but Sean knew this as not so but he also knew that Kelly was a sweet boxer.

After his tea of bacon, sausages and two buttery pieces of home baked soda, Sean climbed the twisty flight of stairs to his bedroom with a full stomach and Eleanor on his mind. Since his twin brother Eddie had left for Art college in London two months before he had ceased regarding this room under the slates as his own. Now it was just somewhere to sleep at weekends, and somewhere to store his clothes and belongings including a pile of boxing magazines, such as 'The Ring', a monthly periodical edited by Nat Fleischer, and a growing collection of long playing records, singles and extended plays.

Sean lay on the bed and stared at the sky blue ceiling. A Sopwith Camel tri-plane with Royal Air Corp roundels banked away to the left. Far above it, coming out of the sun was the famous red Focke Wulf aeroplane of Baron Von Richofen, its Spandaeu machine gun spitting fire. He closed his eyes, and heard Sandy barking in the gloomy yard below.

His dreams took him down on to the floor of a vast ocean. Encased inside the metal shell of a heavy diving suit he looked out of the grilled porthole but could see nothing except trillions

Above the Clouds

of little florescent bubbles dancing inside and outside his head. For the first time in a week he did not dream of Eleanor.

The tap tapping on the bedroom door awoke the student milkman from a deep sleep, and he heard his father's muffled voice saying, "Are you up, Sean?, it's ten past five."

It never occurred to him to rebel, but he had come to dislike the Saturday morning routine, not because he found delivering the milk to the townsfolk boring but because he hated having to collect money from those who found complaints and deceit a natural art form.

"Tell Mrs Loughran she'll get no more milk unless she pays her bill", his father would say, but he just wouldn't do it. Instead he would say to the housewife, "I need a couple of pound off the top or I can't leave you any more milk I'm afraid".

This reluctance on Sean's part and for that matter his father to confront a basic business reality of cash flow was to set in motion a chain of events which was to end tragically.

Later that morning the milkmen drove into Braeside Close, a quadrangle of two and three bedroom council houses in the new Ballygawley Road estate on the western edge of the town. "There's a woman over there in number thirty five who hasn't paid me for months", said the father handing Sean a docket. Charlie McGahan a lad about Sean's age normally helped out on a Saturday but hadn't turned up, and this house was one of his regulars. Sean rapped the door of number thirty five, which was immediately opened by a disarmingly beautiful woman with jet black hair who wore a tight blue skirt and a white v-neck cardigan.

"What have we got here?", she said cheekily, then seeing the milk lorry over Sean's shoulder she continued, "So you're the college student looking for money from a poor girl like myself".

The dimpled smile on her exquisitely made-up face gave her a sultry foreign look and made his heart leap. She stepped back and motioned him into the small working kitchen.

Above a drop-leaf table still littered with breakfast paraphernalia hung a portrait of Padraig Pearse and beside it a framed print of the proclamation of the Irish Republic. Seeing him looking at them, Mary, for that was her name, smiled faintly and took a pound note from a small plastic purse with a silver clasp. She handed Sean the money with the words, "Tell your father that he has left me destitute".

The college student desperately wanted to give her the folded pound back, but instead he just turned and with the scent of her cheap perfume in his nostrils he hurried from the house, nearly knocking her over.

On the northern edge of the town in the townland of Drumcoo was built the first housing estate by the County Council. On Sunday afternoons the young twins, with their mother and younger sister Eileen, would walk out from their home to look at the progress of this large building scheme, which was immediately christened the 'White City'. Hundreds of white painted houses, some with banded brick decoration, fanned out from a large circular green, and access roads like the spokes of a broken bicycle wheel radiated out from its hub at irregular

Above the Clouds

junctions. Saplings of beech, birch and spruce were scatter planted throughout the estate to soften its angular geometry, but they soon succumbed to the wilful attention of street children from the town unused to wide open spaces and country clouds.

The houses were rented by a variety of working people and their families, like bus drivers, joiners, shop assistants, factory workers and caretakers from both religious backgrounds who wanted to escape the mean streets of the town or the muddy lanes of nearby villages. Rows of new houses were given names designed to impress the new inhabitants such as Rossmore Walk, Bernagh Gardens and Drumcoo Green, and from a dwelling in one of these rows a girl called Eleanor, came to live with her parents from England.

A few years later another council estate was built, this time at Mullaghanagh hill on the western fringes of the town. Here however the housing density was much greater and hundreds of red-brick houses were squeezed together into narrow hilly streets not unlike the terraces and lanes which the townsfolk had been persuaded to vacate for health reasons or because of cramped conditions. Homes in Shamble Lane, Greers Terrace, Railway Terrace, Ann Street, Union Place, Sloan Street, and the 'back pens' were abandoned for the new rows of modern houses with inside lavatories. These utilitarian houses removed Catholic families from the centre of the town and relocated them in the west ward, already a predominately Nationalist sector. The estate was unofficially named, 'The Pandarosa', and as the town boundaries expanded and swelled like a blood-filled balloon, so too did the milk run of Park View Dairy. One of the streets in the estate was called Braeside Court, home to Mary, her husband and two small children.

The news from the battle-front was good, 'You're set', said Dino, when he met up with Sean at the electricity board corner later that Saturday afternoon.

'She's mad keen to go out with you', he said with a wide grin, adding 'It took a bit of persuasion at the start, but when I told her about the size of your tool she soon became enthusiastic'.
'You fucker', replied Sean, but his face was flushed with excitement and anticipation at this, his first real date.
'She's coming into town on the seven o'clock bus and you're to meet her in the square opposite the war memorial', announced Dino, pushing and slapping at the happy youth.

The trainee lover made his way down home between the tall houses and shops which leaned out over the street as if to claim their share of the brief autumn sunshine. He stopped at Johnston's drapery store, owned by a Miss Johnston and her bachelor brother called Reggie. Although they owned the shop the hand-painted lettering on the facia board above the door read, 'The Manchester House', and above that suspended from an iron jibbet hung a life-size replica of a sheep. It never dawned on him that this was the symbol par excellence for selling wool to the towns many housewives and frustrated spinsters.

Miss Johnston however was a pleasant and soft spoken spinster with her grey hair tied securely in a bun with the aid of a large tortoise shell comb. Reggie who managed the men's department

was a florid faced man of indeterminate age who always wore a buttoned-up grey cardigan over a check shirt and tweed tie, and shiny brown brogues.
'This is just the tie for you, young sir', said Reggie to Sean, and continued, 'It's the height of fashion, so it is.'

Sean paid seven shillings and sixpence for a slim tie, square-cut at the bottom, with wide horizontal bars of green and blue across it, and hoped it would impress the wonderful Eleanor. Sean and his pals regarded themselves as 'cool dudes', walking fashion statements, and like proud peacocks they continually paraded around the square and the streets leading into it. As luck would have it the east side of the square which included the Ranfurly café caught the afternoon sun, whose bright rays rifled over the stone shoulders of the Ulster Bank and McAleer's Hotel, and reflected off the stuccoed facades and new aluminium framed shop fronts along its entire length.

In the late afternoons when the lengthening shadows dragged their black coats over the paved footpaths, the dudes moved south-west and congregated at the pillar-box which stood at the top of Scotch Street, to take full advantage of the warm sunshine. Here the apprentice gigaloes, resplendent in their rock and roll uniforms of drain-pipe trousers, Italian-style jackets, clean white shirts and slim-jim ties, clamoured like rooks around the blackened chimney-pots of Victorian town houses.

At five minutes to seven that evening a young man wearing a gaudy tie leaned against the iron railings outside Courtney's barber shop and looked around him. He gazed without interest at the familiar patinated outline of the unknown sentinel high up on his stony plinth in the centre of the town square. Shifting his weight from one leg to the other he observed the hands on the clock spire of Wynne's Church move towards the Roman numerals VII and XII. Further down the square he knew that the dudes were assembled at Pagni's chip shop to witness his 'coming of age'.

The terrifying thought that Eleanor might not turn up suddenly occurred to Sean and his entire body shuddered with an involuntary spasm. Then a great shame would engulf him and sweep him away like the Egyptian army in the Red Sea who had followed Moses and the Israelites, or like Cain who slew his brother Abel he would be banished for all eternity to the land of Canaan which is to the east of Eden.

A cold wind sprung up just then and the spire of the Church of St Anne began to totter crazily. Huge blocks of cut sandstone fell earthwards and his eye sockets filled with blood. He raised his hands above his head to protect himself from the toppling masonry and split stonework, and the sweat of terror glistened on his soft skin. With his heart pounding the youth fought with all his strength to regain his composure, and the seconds passed. No-one seemed to have noticed his agitated state. Sean, now calm and composed cocked an eye at the sky and saw that the spire of the church was intact, and the cold wind which had attacked his courage had disappeared.

Above the Clouds

A green UTA bus full of faces drove into the square from Thomas Street and stopped outside Cahoon's jewellery shop. By now the light was fading from the sky but streaks of blue and gold swept upwards from behind the stepped houses which staggered down the hill from the castle. Sean watched as the passengers from Coalisland, Gortin Hill, Edendork and the White City estate spilled out from the rear door of the number forty nine bus.

At first he didn't recognise the smiling woman who alighted last and moved in his direction. In place of the nineteen year old sweet shop assistant was a beautiful creature with lovely eyes, lips an exquisite colour of pink and shapely high-heeled legs. Sean's heart skipped a beat and for a second he hesitated before stepping towards her. They met in the long grey shadow land near the memorial.

'Hello, Sean', said Eleanor politely.

'There's a good picture on in the Astor', replied Sean with a wide grin, hands still deep in the pockets of a sports jacket he had bought recently for its narrow trendy lapels. Eleanor unexpectedly slipped her hand through the crook of his pocketed right arm and wheeling round they crossed the square in an endless matter of fact sort of way. Warm meaty odours drifted from the open door of McAleer's Hotel as the couple, for that's what they were, passed by. The gathering of dudes saw them approach and from their ranks came a series of low wolf whistles followed by muttered curses of admiration.

'Christ, what a body', someone gasped, as Sean and his embarrassed sweetheart turned into Irish Street. The smiling youth knew that the next day, after mass, he would be required to render an elaborate and exaggerated account of his amorous adventures to the assembled dudes.

Sean was a little uneasy at the forward way Eleanor had linked him and found himself adjusting his stride to accommodate her shorter steps. Though he walked in his own patch in his own town, the clip of a second set of footsteps on the pavement beside him was a bit unnerving. About half way down the twisting disorderly street of sprawling grocery stores, tiny huckster shops and houses of intoxication, Sean caught the hawkish eye of one Joseph Stewart, member of parliament for East Tyrone, public house proprietor, auctioneer and undertaker.

Dressed in a brown tweed three-piece suit with silk pocket handkerchief and a spotted dickie-bow he stared from the door of his pub at the approaching young couple with wry amusement. Sean knew that his father who frequented the pub would soon be told of his eldest son's company keeping.

As they passed by Sean was sure he heard the elderly spiv singing a George Formby ditty,
"I'm standing by the lamp-post at the corner of the street
Until a certain little lady comes by
Oh me, oh my, I hope that little lady comes by".

In the darkness of the cinema, he said,
"You've got a beautiful name", and she laughed quietly.

Above the Clouds

"Where do you come from?" Eleanor whispered in his ear, and he told her that he had been stolen by the gypsies as a child. In his minds eye Homer's horse of Troy sprouted wings, broke into a wooden gallop and flew up into a silver sky. Sitting in the back row of the balcony Sean put his arm around her neck and felt her nestle softly against him. Her silky hair brushed his cheek and an unknown fragrance filled his nostrils and invaded his senses. Looping fingertips touched Eleanor's eyelids and long eye lashes, and he wanted to look deep into her eyes, but she gently removed his hand and smiled without taking her eyes of the screen. She calmly accepted his admiration and took his longing looks to herself, while he began to drift and lose himself in the maze of her hair. Against her knees he wanted to lie like an animal looking for warmth and affection.

After the pictures were over the teenage couple hurried back up to the market square in time for Eleanor to catch the ten fifteen bus to Coalisland via Newmills, though in truth she only lived a mile from the town centre, but the October evening had turned cold and rain was in the air. She did not link him this time, which was a bit of a relief but held his hand as he gallantly moved to the outside of the pavement. Sean desperately wanted to kiss her and knew by the way she looked at him and the way she leaned her head back a little so that he could see the soft nape of her neck that she liked him. With no bus in sight they leaned against the dark wall of the jeweller's shop and he slipped his arm around her waist. As he kissed her lightly on the lips her eyes widened and the building seemed to stagger in the empty air. He kissed her again, and she gasped a little as if she was out of breath. The bus drew up and stepping from the shadows she thanked him politely for a wonderful evening, and joined a small queue of some ten people for the homeward journey. With a shudder the bus drove out towards quieter country roads leaving the square full of shadows and Sean swallowed hard, the taste of her lips lingering in his dry mouth.

Father and son rarely spoke to one another now, not that there was any antagonism between them, it was just that as a generation apart they had little to say to one another except for mundane conversation. But Sean had watched from the vantage point of youth as his father gradually began to take on the flattened angular look of the stone walls that surrounded their property while the joints in his body began filling with cement.

Weeds grew in the empty yard between the cracked concrete, and were rampant on the side of the paths leading to the dairy. Ragwort and stinging nettles flourished on piles of brick rubble that lay where they fell when an old byre wall had collapsed in on itself. The tops of the high walls harboured glorious milky specimens of dandylions oblivious to the wind that raked them with murderous hailstones. Sean felt pity for the Victorian artisans who had laboured so skilfully when the property was built to see it now being systematically stripped of its pride by a relentless and aggressive neglect.

Four hours on a Sunday morning took care of the milk run, a scampering scramble of deliveries when the lorry criss-crossed the streets and the looping outer roads of the town like paint dribbled across a Jackson Pollock canvas. Charlie McGahan who helped out at the weekends was a good harmonica player and Irish dancer, and he and Sean became firm friends.

Charlie often quizzed Sean about Irish history and one afternoon as they were unloading crates from the lorry he suddenly declared himself to be a republican socialist. This announcement coincided with the painting of a large blue flag complete with the starry plough in white which appeared mysteriously on a gable wall near the railway station. By eleven o'clock Sean, his father and Charlie returned to the dairy, and went up to the house where a breakfast of tea, toast and hard boiled eggs awaited them.

This was followed by the ritual of twelve thirty mass in the Gothic extravagance of St Patrick's church. The seats were hard in this church packed with people rich and poor, but the splendour of its dusty interior made the humourless sermons bearable to the young church-goer, whose eyes roamed over the hammer-beam roof, marble reredos and magnificent stained glass windows.

The Convent of Mercy nuns in their black habits and starched white bibs filtered into their reserved seats on the side aisle in front of Our Lady's altar. Sean looked for the small bowed figure of Mother Aloysious, an aunt of his father's who had entered the convent as a seventeen year old postulant many years before and had given piano lessons to generations of the town's aspiring children. She had forsaken her own name of Winifred in favour of some male saint and when her diminutive frame shuffled past, the former altar boy lowered his head and stared at his feet.

After mass the dudes were waiting for the Casanova kid in Pagni's chip shop. As they sipped hot orange drinks from glasses decorated with pink mermaids, 'Hannibal' said, 'Well, did you get it?'

'Get what?' parried Sean
'You know what I mean, you asshole', laughed Hannibal.
'Did you give her one?' blurted out Harry.
'Did you even lay a hand on her?' asked a shocked Alec.
'From where I was looking, he was getting on very well', interjected Dino, the film projectionist and man about town.

Sometimes on a Sunday after dinner Sean would walk out towards the Black Lough in the hours before he caught the eight thirty train which took him and hordes of chattering nurses, student teachers, and trainee civil servants back to the dark streets of Belfast. On this particular evening he left the house, his shoes shining and strode out from the town with the spire of St Anne's at his back. As he walked he became aware of the faint odours of cattle which hung in the air at the side of the twisting roads with their high sprawling hedges. As he came round a narrow corner before the road widened out towards O'Brien's hill he almost collided with someone meandering in the opposite direction.

Above the Clouds

"That the second time you've nearly knocked me down", the voice said, and Sean found himself looking into the dark eyes, wide smile of flashing white teeth and crimson lips of Mary from number thirty five Braeside Close.

He had called at the house the day before for the milk money but as there was no reply from his knocking he dropped the bill through the letter-box.

"She's skating on thin ice", his father had said when he returned to the lorry empty handed, and went on, "that's three months money she owes, and I can't see how she's going to pay it with two small children in the house and a waster of a husband who spends all his time in the bookies. Boys like him haven't the slightest intention of ever doing a day's work in their lives". Mary laughed in a carefree sort of way, and rubbed her elbow.

"What brings you out by the Lough?" she asked. "A young fella like you should be looking for girls around the town instead of bumping into lonely married women", continued the town's answer to Jane Russell.
Sean stared for a second at this tall, beautiful woman with the hour-glass figure and reckoned that she was about twenty five years old, before muttering, "Sorry".
"That's all right", laughed Mary again, and brushing past him she lightly touched his arm with her fingers, and was gone.

Sean stood still for some time in the tranquillity of the evening and wondered at what she had said until the gathering gloom brushed over his shoes and stole their polish. He turned back towards the town and noticed how the stony church spire still pointed heavenwards but its bulk was taking on the transubstantiation of a Monet canvas.

He reached the front door of his house as the light failed but stayed for a few minutes in the gloom even though it was getting cold, and closely examined the stuccoed walls on either side of the door. Then slowly and deliberately he sort of retreated into the shelter of the dark doorway. Sean paused for a moment in the hall, his thoughts slow and confused, and in the back of his head he heard a distant faint growling which gradually grew louder until a mighty roar almost split his eardrums.

4

It was a cold autumn evening and the spires, towers and chimney stacks of the town huddled together in smoky disorder against a ragged sky as Sean moved out from the deep shadow of the cenotaph to meet Eleanor. Her blond hair was pinned back in a pony tail which made her look taller and daintier, though her pink ear-rings made her ears seem unusually prominent. The chocolate and candy girl was wearing a brown sheepskin coat that belonged to her older sister and when Sean told her she looked sophisticated Eleanor blushed and seemed flustered by the remark. As the couple passed Donnelly's greengrocer shop on their way to the cinema, for they were now going out together for about a month, Sean began humming the hit song, 'Wooden Heart' by Elvis 'The King' Presley.

"Treat me nice, treat me cool, treat me like the way you should, for I'm not made of wood and I don't have a wooden heart", he sang.

Eleanor smiled at her young beau and Sean felt happy and contented, or at least he thought he did, for this feeling of wellbeing was a rare phenomenon for someone who should be rebelling against the ordinariness of life. His weekly lectures in Belfast had left him with the impression that to experience joy was to betray philosophers like Decartes, but he reasoned that the little piece of earth he inhabited was his to do with as he pleased.

That night as they waited for the bus Eleanor shyly told her that she loved him and would always love him. This unexpected declaration took Sean aback and he wanted to tell her also that he loved her but he couldn't utter the words so instead he just kissed her.

That Saturday morning however as he was cutting the top off a hard boiled egg at the breakfast table his father spoke to him from behind the pages of the Irish News.

"Who's the young lassie you're knocking about with these days?"

The tone of his voice was incisive but its slightly raised pitch sent our warning signals that a glib answer would be less than adequate. He lowered the paper and before Sean could answer, for he had been expecting the question now for a few weeks, continued, "I'm told her father, whose a Yorkshire man, is a production manager down in the glass fabrics".

The father folded the paper neatly and looked at his silent son.

"The English are a funny lot, and I should know. I've dealt with plenty of them during the war, in the cattle trade around the west Riding of Yorkshire. They'd believe anything you told them, a naïve lot for the most part, but there's a directness about them that you won't find here."

He pushed back the chair and got up from the table, saying, "I used to know a girl in Skipton, she worked in the Red Lion Hotel."

Then he stopped talking and Sean looked up at his father and said, "Her name is Eleanor". Faint lights from a distant star were reflected in both their eyes as the two men headed down the yard to the lorry and the awaiting town beyond the walls of sculpted stone.

The glass fabrics, or to give it its proper name, 'Turner Brothers & Newell', produced bolts of synthetic yarn by the thousand. The parent factory was somewhere in the north of England, and Alec, one of the dudes, who now worked in the 'fabrics' knew Eleanor's dad. He told Sean that Sam as he was called, had come over here from Rochdale in Lancashire along with several others to help train a new workforce, and shortly after that they and their families had settled here.

The factory itself was a rectangular stone building with massive windows divided into hundreds of small glazed squares that captured the sunlight in its glassy embrace. Passengers and porters who stood on the platforms of the nearby railway station at Beechvalley could glimpse its blue slated roof above a canopy of mature trees lining both banks of a small river that flowed out past Major Dickson's weaving sheds and blackened brick chimney stacks. Here and there among the burned bricks were a few with pale red, orange and even blue blemishes on their smooth skins.

The five days he spent in Belfast every week seemed to the aspiring philosopher as just the backdrop to the real life he lived in his home town.

Around mid-day the following Saturday the milk lorry turned into the Ballygawley Road estate from the Windmill hill and stopped between two rows of identical houses, their roofs festooned with television aerials. Sean rapped the door of number thirty five Braeside Close.

"Countess Markevich, I presume", he heard himself say when the door was opened by Mary whose lips were painted the deepest vermilion. He was astonished by his cheek and candour.

"You're some boy", Mary's lips said. "You'll be trying it on with me before long, the way you're going."

The student walked into the small kitchen and Mary closed the door behind him, leaning cheekily against it, a dish-cloth in one hand.

"Can you see enough", she laughed as their eyes met but not before he knew that for the split second his pupils had lingered on the ample thrust of her full breasts they had betrayed his desire for her.

"There's plenty to see", he said lamely and looking past her he saw that the picture of Padraig Pearse was hanging at an angle on the woodchip wall. "Your hero's a bit crooked", he added.

Above the Clouds

Ignoring his words she said chirpily, "I saw you at the pictures last Saturday night with your wee girlfriend." The word 'wee' stung him, and he lied in reply "she's not my girlfriend".
"Well the way you two were going at it I'd say she was a very close friend."
"Never mind about that", he replied abruptly, "I've a milk bill here that needs seeing to".

Mary ignored the summons, and said, "I'll be out around the lough tomorrow evening about seven and you never know we might bump into one another again, and you can tell me all about your sweety shop helper!"

At that she gave Sean a playful swish with the dish-cloth, but he caught hold of it and tugged hard. They both sort of fell against the sink, Mary grabbing him with both arms and laughingly shrieked, "You cheeky bastard".

The feel of her body against him was exhilarating and wondrous, and with their arms still locked together she whispered, "lend me a couple of quid till next week, I'm really skint".

Mary stepped back from him and pulling at the strap of her bra and moving her shoulders back and forward she readjusted herself. Sean took a folded five pound note from the back pocket of his jeans and handed it to her. He had seen a little silver cross and chain in McQueen's jewellers shop opposite his house and had intended to buy it as a surprise for Eleanor that evening, but now this beautiful woman both thrilled and terrorised him. Sean, sweating in the heavy gold-brocaded jacket of the matador, his muleta trailing in the sand, walked slowly back to the safety of the lorry with the roar of the crowd in the Barcelona bullring singing in his ears as it had for Manolo Bienvenidia in Hemingway's novel 'Death in the Afternoon'. Charlie McMahon gave him a knowing look when he got into the cab, and his father said, "Did she give you anything?

"She did", Sean replied and continued, "she gave me three quid so she did". "Well something is better than nothing I suppose", his father answered, and as an afterthought said, "she's a chancy bit of goods, that one, if you ask me".

Sean left the house on a raw Saturday evening in October singing snatches from Nat 'King' Cole's ballad September Song.

"The autumn leaves drift by your window
The autumn leaves of green and gold ..." he warbled, but the sound of his voice in the unusual quietness of the street caused him to stop for a second before he turned up the hill towards the square. But a frown came over his face because he had forgotten some of the lyrics.

"And the days tumble down to a precious few", it didn't sound right he thought looking up at the sky with its streaky horizontal bands of orange, red and purple. It was cold but there was no rain, and Sean walked slowly and deliberately with his hands thrust deep into his trouser pockets as if that would help him recall the words of the song.

Above the Clouds

There had been occasions over the last few weeks when he had loved Eleanor wildly. He would often think about her during lectures in Belfast when men in black gowns droned on and on about the remarkable creativity of children, facts which every student around him already knew having been children themselves. The thought of her made him tremble, but he was troubled for he knew that his feelings for her were changing. Her politeness and acceptance of everything he said, coupled with the quaintness of her fading English accent had begun to bore him. He was also getting rather fed up of having to lie to the dudes about his sexual adventures, for in truth they were largely non-existent. Kissing and cuddling was all very well but like the young bulls in O'Brien's field he was anxious to prove his manhood.

People tumbled from the seven o'clock bus but Eleanor was not among them and Sean stood for a few seconds in the chilly air unsure of himself. The disappointed young singer felt a strange finality when the bus departed round the corner of Thomas Street, and he looked without interest at a girl in a duffle coat who crossed the square from the library and vanished behind the recently cleaned memorial plinth made ready to receive its pointless offering of poppy wreaths.

Sean looked at the shrinking road as it twisted and looped up the hill on the way to nowhere, and half remembered a line from D.H. Lawrence's great novel, The Rainbow, that "the great home of the soul is the open road."

A light veil of mist crowned the woody slopes of the hill that ran down to the Lough.

"Fancy seeing you", laughed Mary recklessly as Sean suddenly appeared before her on the road. Her coolness and confidence excited him so he just took her hand and said, "There's a short-cut up through the trees that we can take."

A cool breeze started up but he felt nothing as they stumbled hand and hand up a stony path between dark boughs of conifer. The light had almost gone from the sky by the time they reached a grassy knoll on the hilltop. Mary lay back in the long grass and Sean bent down to her. Her tight burgundy coloured blouse burst open like the skin of an over-ripe plum as she arched her back to greet his taut torso, and in the dimming of the evening a pearly light radiated around them.

He kissed her arms, her neck, her throat, her hard nipples in a frenzy of virginal passion until trickles of sweat from his body ran like a mountain stream down into the deep valley between her glacial breasts. Firm hands guided his buttery fingers down into the deep silkiness of her thighs as she cried out and called to him in a language as old as Darwin's theory of evolution. Groping and fumbling in an ecstasy of desire the trainee skydiver tugged his ripcord amid the sound of rolling thunder as an adrenalin rush as high as the sky, above swept him into her yielding embrace.

A milli-second later his gushing seed having overflowed like milky semolina from a hot saucepan cooled and slowed as it enveloped her suspenders and the tops of her nyloned legs. In

Above the Clouds

that instant he felt both humiliated and ashamed as Mary sat up and grabbed the tail-end of his shirt, carefully ironed only a few hours earlier by his mother, and used it to wipe the semen from her inner legs. "Don't worry about it", she whispered to the aviator and smiling added, "It could happen to a bishop."

Shakily, he stood up, his clothes covered in grass and leaves and the chill of an autumn evening on his quivering buttocks. In summer evenings he had seen lovers cross the fields below him and go down to the water to lie among ferns and foxgloves, but now spits of rain began to fall with an urgent pitter patter on the leaves above him, and larger droplets were staining the glacial stones on the path beside him.

"Let's get out of here before we get a soaking", said Mary, disturbing his reverie and pushed him like a reluctant calf before her. They clambered over an iron gate onto a narrow road just as darkness fell and giggling and cuddling the lovers stole back into town just as the lights of the street standards were switched on. Sean left Mary and walked quickly down the hill keeping close to the stone wall that swept all the way round to the station entrance for a cold curtain of rain had swung down over the town from the east. In any case he didn't want to be seen for having just committed the sin of adultery he needed time to re-assemble his thoughts.

He crossed over the metal bridge plastered with showband posters and up past a string of closed public houses packed with whispering men, his father included, who enjoyed downing the forbidden liquor on the Sabbath.

This part of the road was called Lower Scotch Street and ran parallel to the walled market yard where two modest entrances had been punched in its solid flanks. Market day was on a Tuesday and from early morning the air was filled with the bellowing of cattle continually prodded and slapped by hard faced men in red boots and armed with knotted ash plants. Facing the yard were about a dozen assorted buildings which constituted the street proper, five of which were public houses. Pat Marley's, originally the Commercial Hotel, was the first pub at the low corner. Then came Owen McKee's followed by Miss Quinn's, a dark barrack of a place, and next was Mallon's with their name picked out in small coloured tiles on the entrance step, and lastly at the top end stood Packie Quinn's pub. Slotted between them were a variety of businesses which depended for their existence on the farmers of Killybrackey, Brantry, Mulbuoy, Dernasaor and Mullaghmore.

There was McCooey's eating house, O'Neill's tiny confectionery shop, Moorhead's post office and paper shop, Trotters hardware store, Finnegan's shoe-shop and P Cush & Co, Solicitors. Some of the outhouses in the sloping yards behind the buildings had been rented out, and there Johnny Loughran repaired cars. Fairburn's hatched chickens in large incubators, and Charlie McCord printed stationery, including wedding invitations and business cards from a shed roofed with asbestos slates and called 'The Excelsior Press'.

McKee's was the favourite watering hole of Sean's father and on most Saturday nights he was to be found there drinking Powers whiskey and bottles of stout in a small snug with several of his cronies. The procedure was usually repeated on Sunday afternoons, the drink tasting all the sweeter because of the strict licensing laws. On more than one occasion Sean had been summoned by his mother with the words, "Go down to McKee's and tell that father of yours that his dinner is on the table. If he's not up for it in five minutes it's for the bin".

Sean pushed open the yard gate and entered the fortress, the light in the front room window told him where the family had gathered. Letting himself in quietly he went straight to the kitchen for he was wet, hungry and worried.

He did not have to return to Belfast that night for he was about to begin a four week practice as a student teacher at his old primary school run by the Presentation Brothers. All of the Brothers were southerners, the principal Brother Oliver was a Tipperary man, and Brother Raymond hailed from County Cork, like his mother. Every week day morning his father still stacked milk crates again the side wall of the school near the front door, and each crate held forty one-third pint bottles. On Monday mornings a cardboard box of straws was left on top of the crates. The milk was supplied courtesy of the Government and any left over was drank by the hungry greyhounds that evening.

After a cup of tea and a sausage sandwich Sean lay on his bed and switched on radio Luxembourg.

"People see us everywhere, they think you really care, but myself I can't deceive, I know it's only make believe", sang Conway Twitty on fabulous 208.

Sean closed his eyes and felt his body begin to shake and tingle with a blood gorged passion for Mary, a juicy Eve with silky skin and breasts like ripe pears.

"Oh my sweet Lord", he muttered to himself, falling asleep under a sky full of aircraft. The young aviator dreamed that he was flying high but maybe he was just falling.

The morning was cold and clear when Sean strode into the school yard of his youth. Brother Oliver, in black suit, white clerical collar and gold fainne beamed at him from the top of the concrete steps at the front entrance. They shook hands warmly, "Good man, yourself, it's nice to see you again", he said and added as an aside, "I'll be able to get in a bit of golfing practice now that you're here".

Climbing the stairs to the fourth year classroom Sean looked down into the playground from a large metal-framed window carelessly painted with white gloss. Stevie Bloomfield would never have tolerated such sloppiness he thought. Stacked neatly by the wall below him were a dozen milk crates on the top of which sat a box of straws with the words Parkview Dairy clearly printed in maroon on the top. The fledgling school master continued up the stairs, his polished shoes echoing on the well-worn timbers.

Sean spent the day sharpening pencils with a pen-knife, blowing on a chrome whistle,

Above the Clouds

collecting dog-eared exercise books, mixing powder paint and in the process circling endless miles around a room full of thirty three chirpy squabbling boys.

"And how's your mother these days?", enquired Brother Raymond later that day as they patrolled the play yard during dinner time. He spoke more out of politeness than interest, but before Sean could answer he added, "Does your father still race the greyhounds? I saw him out over O'Brien's hill the other day with a couple of brindle pups." His next remarks betrayed his real interest for he said, "He always keeps a good dog, does your father. Let me know if any of them are racing down in the Oaks Park and I might have me a little wager or two."

With that he tapped his nose twice with his right index finger and gave Sean a little wink. A sudden commotion at the far end of the yard near the wall with the convent school made them turn around to see two boys punching at each other.

"That's McRory at it again", said Brother Raymond but made no move in their direction, and then said, "He's turning into a bit of a bully, and I'd cane him only he's a good singer and I need him for the feis choir."

That evening a jaded student made his way down a wet street from the confines of his home and rounded the corner into Georges Street. The rain had crept almost unnoticed into the hilly streets of the town and as he passed Wherry's Hotel its soft sheet swept over him flecking the lighted porch with its dark watery stains. By the time Sean had walked the few hundred yards to the tiled steps of the art Deco cinema he felt uncomfortably wet. Dino, film projectionist, dude and man about town was waiting for him.

"I've got a message for you, from sexy Eleanor", he said smiling, a cigarette dangling from his lower lip in imitation of Humphrey Bogart.

"Let's have it then", said Sean, trying to disguise the sudden rise in the pitch of his voice.

Dino seemed not to notice, but nevertheless made no answer and turning walked into the empty brightly light foyer, where a large poster advertised the film, 'Summer Holiday', starring Cliff Richard and featuring Hank Marvin and the Shadows.

"What did she say, you twisted fucker?" shouted Sean after him. Dino skipped up the narrow stone steps to the projection room behind the balcony, pursued by an animated Sean.

"Give me a hand with these cans of film and I'll tell you, if you can control yourself", said Dino.

"You're a bit of an asshole", muttered Sean as together the pals began to load a reel of film on to the large spool of the main projector.

"She said she as very sorry about last Saturday night, but her aunt and uncle were over from England and she had to go out with them", said Dino.

"So it's all right to leave me in the lurch?" grumbled Sean.

Above the Clouds

"It's time you got a telephone in your house and maybe then I wouldn't have to carry messages from your little Protestant girlfriend", said Dino opening another can of film.
"I don't care what religion she is", interrupted Sean, but Dino continued, "Aye, you mightn't but I'll bet your aul fella and aul doll are hardly over the moon about it. Anyway it's your life but if you want to take her to the pictures on Saturday night you'd better see her pronto. If I were you I'd check her out at the sweet shop tomorrow, otherwise some other brandy ball will be humping her by this time next week".
"You mean you're desperate to nail her yourself", laughed Sean aiming a kick at Dino's crotch.
"I'm not into imports", smirked Dino, "I've enough local produce to keep me going till Christmas".
"So you say", replied Sean.
Slamming shut the chrome side of the cinematic machine Dino turned to his friend and said, "Let's play a couple of records before we go".

From the pile of singles on the table beside the record player Sean picked up 'Half way to Paradise', by Billy Fury and 'The crowd' by Roy Orbison.

The town clock struck twelve on Saturday the third of November as the Parkview Dairy lorry drove towards the Pandarosa. A biting east wind was blowing in from the Steppes of Russia as Sean and Charlie rode shotgun on the back of the lorry. Even though it was bitterly cold they preferred to sit on upturned crates in the rear where they could chat freely, and of course they kept an eagle eye open for any renegade Indians who might have broken out of their reservation near Fort Apache.

"Thanks for the book on James Connolly", Charlie said, "Ireland could have been the first socialist country in the world if it hadn't have been for the bloody Brits". He paused and continued, "We'll never be free unless there's another revolution".

Sean made no reply, and mistaking his silence for acquiesce Charlie went on, "There's a republican meeting tomorrow night, and your invited to come along, if you want".

At that moment Sean's father stuck his capped head out of the lorry window, saying "Are you pair going to collect any money this side of the new year or what?"

In the small kitchen under the stern gaze of Padraig Pearse Sean fumbled with the straps of Mary's bra as her luscious lips sucked and pummelled the yielding skin around his mouth, nose and cheeks. He could feel the perspiration on his forehead as this Venus, this Helen of Troy, this Cleopatra withdrew her lips suddenly from his and pushed him away with a smile of steel. When she suggested that he should pay off the entire milk bill for her Sean just nodded.

"See you tomorrow evening by the Lough, if you like", she said opening the door, but the crestfallen lover felt for the first time the terrible weight of his great sin. Carrying the burden of his secret affair with him like a man lifting a hundred weight of coal on his back, he crossed the road to the lorry.

Above the Clouds

"You look like you've been sucking a gobstopper", said Charlie with a sly wink.

Part of the old dairy beside the cold store had been ingenuously converted into a pigeon loft by lifting off the corrugated roof and raising it on top of fencing poles which were then boarded round with lengths of tongued and grooved floor boards. Redundant milk crates found new uses as nesting boxes for the cooing birds. During the summer months Sean's father and Herbie Johnston, now a member of the police reserve, would sit together under a knarled and cankerous pear tree. Year after year it still produced a crop of small hard pears whose skins were diffused with a pinky wash where the sun had managed to struggle above the snow capped granite peaks that hid the yard from an inquisitive world. There the two men would wait in patient expectation to clock the homing birds who fell from the skies like American Mustang planes landing on aircraft carriers in the south China seas. Thousands of pigeons were released weekly from their massed hampers in locomotive yards on the outskirts of towns such as Skerries, Arklow, Waterford, Haversford West and Penzance to navigate their way home across shimmering estuaries, smoky towns, fields of corn and oats and meandering rivers.

By now the season was virtually over except for one last race. The coveted Bude Cup was an open competition for birds of all ages and was the highlight of the fanciers calendar in Northern Ireland. Only the best pigeons were entered as they had to contend with two seas, the Bristol channel and the Irish sea, and next Saturday the tenth of November was the date of the big race.

Pigeons were far from Sean's mind as he stood in front of a Victorian swivel mirror in his parents' bedroom that evening. He combed his blond hair with great care smoothing and arranging a little quiff expertly with his fingers. He was conscious of how well his new Buddy Holly style glasses complimented his appearance. The provincial beau stood back from the mirror and surveyed himself with no little satisfaction. He practiced smiling at himself eventually settling for a grimace that he had seen on the face of Elvis Presley in the film 'GI Blues' and he intended to try it out on Eleanor in a few minutes time.

At five minutes to seven Sean stepped into the cold night air, his hand protecting his precious quiff from a swirling wind. He looked up just as the moon disappeared behind the saw-toothed silhouette of the houses which stretched up the paved hill adjacent to him. He was anxious to see Eleanor again for he was stunned by her prettiness and her shapely-ness, and he knew from the start by the way she laughed at what he said that she liked how he talked to her. And of course her declaration of love thrilled him.

The street was still full of people of all ages and the lights from the shop windows lit up the wonder in their faces. Sean fended off a couple of hello's as he made his way into the widening expanse of the town square.

"Hello", he said, giving Eleanor his best Elvis-like smile as they met on the pavement opposite the cenotaph.

Above the Clouds

"Hello yourself", Eleanor replied and then added, "you look like you're man up there in the uniform".

The remark wounded the young pretender, and as their eyes met he said, "What did those boyos ever achieve? The Enniskillings and the Royal Irish were little more than cannon fodder – mugs who served the British establishment."

The words just came tumbling from his lips, and many more besides in a vehement outburst that surprised both of them. "What's got into you all of a sudden", said Eleanor anxiously, and then said, "you'll be blaming me next for all the troubles in this part of the world. I thought you told me that three of your mother's brothers served in the Merchant Navy during the last war?"

"So they did", came the reply, "but soldiers are different".

Then remembering that he was on a date Sean saluted smartly and gave his girl a real forgive-me-please smile.

"Your hair looks nice", she said.

"So does yours", said Sean softly without even looking.

In the intimate half light of the picture house Sean's eyes continually drifted away from the screen and onto the firm outline of Eleanor's buttoned blouse. Her breasts rose and fell in harmony with the regularity of her breathing. He had only ever kissed her unlike his sexual adventure with Mary, and yet he knew that he loved her in a star-spangled sort of way. The desire for her continually tortured him and sometimes he even felt like screaming. Bernini's marble masterpiece, 'The agony of St Theresa', floated before him and he thought he was going to be sick. In his loneliness and confusion he pressed her hand, and whispered in her ear that he loved her. As their fingers intertwined Eleanor pulled him close and replied, "You're my pretty boy Floyd".

Sean spent most of the afternoon of Sunday the fourth of November in Pagni's chip shop with the dudes, playing records on the juke-box. He played Conway twitty's version of Mona Lisa four times in succession much to the annoyance of other patrons, and he decided against taking a walk out by the Black Lough.

On Friday evening the ninth of November a tired Sean who had just finished his second week of teaching practice, ambled down to the dairy just as Geordie Benson was delivering the bottled milk to the refrigerated store. Geordie who worked part time for Killyman Co-operative as a driver was also in the police reserve. Like most of the co-op employees he was a small farmer who lived in the rushy town land of Listamlet, and being in the Orange Order there wasn't much going on in the countryside that he didn't know about. On the previous Saturday night Sean had run into George and his wife as he was coming out of the picture house with Eleanor. Geordie had nudged his wife and laughingly said, "It's way past your bedtime young fella". Sean blushed.

Above the Clouds

On Saturday morning the tenth of November pigeons were on everyone's mind and the weather was favourable as light winds and little rain was forecast for the English Channel. Sean, Charlie and his father grafted hard all morning and when the lorry drove in to the inner sanctum about one o'clock Herbie Johnston was standing by the loft, the spikly ends of his white hair forming a sort of Byzantine halo around his head.

"Well John", said Herbie, "this is it. This is the day! It's just the ticket for us".
"Aye, and for anybody else with a good bird", replied Sean's father grudgingly.

Just then Herbie caught sight of Charlie, who had begun stacking empty crates on a low concrete platform beside the cold store, and his body seemed to stiffen for a second. As they walked up the yard Sean overheard Herbie say to his father, "How long has that fella been working for you?" The reply came, "On and off for a couple of months. He helps me out mostly at weekends and he's useful to have about the place".
"He's useful all right", muttered Herbie darkly.

A message however awaited the pigeon men. Sean's father picked up a telegram from the kitchen table and read it aloud. "Birds held over till Sunday, stop, fog in channel, stop".

At five thirty on the morning of armistice Sunday Sean and his dad loaded the milk crates on to the lorry using a long iron hook. Normally they did not speak to one another as there was no need, but this morning under a scattering of stars Sean sensed his father's excitement and said, "I suppose the birds will be liberated at first light".

The father of the young man with the blond hair paused and replied, "Aye, they'll be on their way soon. If we get a move on we can get that lazy sod Charlie out of his bed and get back here before ten. Your mother may have to go to mass without us today, but Herbie will be here anyway for he's getting off duty a bit early because of the parade to the cenotaph".

Sean was surprised when his father added, "Boys like him have it easy. All they do is get well paid for wandering the roads in uniform and hassling law abiding citizens".

Charlie and his older brother Jack lived with their widowed mother in a council bungalow on the Donaghmore Road. For some time now Charlie who used to be a good riser had to be dragged from his bed by his mother, and sure enough when Sean rapped the kitchen window about five forty five Charlie was only getting dressed. As the footsteps of the two young men echoed on the concrete path, Sean said, "Jesus Christ, the father will give you the run if you don't wise up".

"I'm only in the bed about ten minutes, and I had to climb in the bloody back window", replied Charlie.

"Where the hell were you?" queried Sean, adding hopefully, "are you giving some lassie what for?" "No way", replied Charlie as they reached the lorry and, looking Sean straight in the eye, said, "I was on manoeuvres, if you must know".

— 44 —

Above the Clouds

Sean's father had used his friendship with Joseph Stewart MP to secure a contract to supply the new hospital with milk and this was one of their first calls. The eight storey block of glass, steel and concrete stood at the top of the Quarry Lane hill and looked like a gigantic perforated bandage. As the dairymen drove into its orb the glow from the interior cast long parallel shafts of light into the frosty air that would have warmed the cold heart of Le Corbusier, but to the ant-like patients its brutish presence and enormous geometry was unnerving.

"You look like you've been pulled through a hedge backwards", said the father to Charlie, who was busy blowing warm air into his cupped hands.
"He's been up half the night with indigestion", said Sean.

"What you need to do, is to drink down a pint of milk. That will settle down your stomach", said the man who had a cure for everything.
"A raw egg with it would be even better", he added.

There was no response from either Charlie or Sean as the lorry rattled to a halt outside the kitchen door of the South Tyrone hospital. The lads dragged eight full crates along the wet tiled floor of the kitchen and into an icy store full of red jelly in stainless steel bowls and shelves stacked with sausages, sides of bacon and loops of black pudding. Outside the kitchen they shared a couple of slices of cooked ham deftly removed from a large plate near the cooker and washed it down with a bottle of milk between them.

Then without a word they took their places on the running board, one on each side of the lorry, ready to do battle, their polished lances at the ready. As the vehicle moved steadily towards town and along Thomas Street, Carland Road and Castlefields, these young knights of the road would drop off at intervals, armed only with small crates and running over frosty lawns, would deposit creamy measures outside the doors of pregnant women, fitful infants and snoring couples. When the lorry slowed to a walk they jumped on again, reloading as it quickened and prepared themselves for a forage into the side streets and narrow alleyways of the town proper.

By seven fifty they were deep into enemy territory and from the turret of their Sherman tank they saw the unguarded back of the bronze sentinel come into view. On this, Remembrance Sunday, the square was bedecked with union flags as the troop commander parked his tank and walked into Sloan's newsagents. Sean was momentarily startled when in the gathering light a tired voice behind him said, "Give us a pint there will you?".

Turning round Sean found his way blocked by a black police car, which had noiselessly glided up almost to where he stood beside the lorry. Charlie was nowhere to be seen so the young gunner placed a pint of milk in the outstretched hand of the police driver. Then he heard his father's voice saying, "You boys look like you could do with a cup of tea".

When the car disappeared into the greyness of the hill above the square his father said to his son, "You never know when you might need a favour."

Above the Clouds

At five minutes to eight the lorry parked opposite an elegant Georgian terrace in Northland Row and the three occupants made their way into a freezing cold church. Sean stood at the back of a side aisle and leant against a massive fine-tooled block-stone pillar. The dimly lit interior seemed full of poor people, insomniacs and nurses made grotesque by the ghostly shadows thrown from the tapering flames of the many candles.

Angels, saints and crucifixes crowded the walls between the gothic window insets and the ornately carved confessional boxes. The bell rang and he heard the priest, dressed in purple and gold robes intone, "Me culpa, mea culpa, mea maxima culpa".

Sean counted again the twenty four beams supporting the roof coupling and in his minds eye marvelled at the Michelangelo frescoes that adorned the Sistine Chapel in Rome.

At the communion bell Sean saw his father rise from a pew and genuflect. He followed him out of the church, dipping his right index finger into the holy water font and made a perfunctory sign of the cross. Charlie was huddled in the cab of the lorry, fast asleep.

At five minutes to ten the men of the Fianna reigned in their weary steeds and dismounted. A stiff breeze had blown an old newspaper into an ancient fairy thorn bush that grew in the corner of their mountain retreat. Herbie, still in his police uniform was seated in an old armchair facing the pigeon loft with a tartan blanket wrapped around his ample frame. On the ground beside him lay his helmet, its distinctive badge of a harp entwined with shamrocks beneath a crown caught and reflected the light. Poking out from beneath it was his snub-nose revolver and leather holster.

Herbie rose out of the armchair with a huge yawn and to Sean he looked like the blanketed bulk of Balzac sculpted by the great Rodin. He gestured to the warriors saying, "Away and get yourselves a bit of a feed and I'll keep an eye out for the birds, and tell the missus to send me down a good mug of strong tea for it would skin the balls off a monkey."

Some ten minutes later Sean approached the dozing figure of Herbie with the steaming tea. Uncertain, he sat the mug down on the ground beside the pigeon clock, and retreated to his lonely garret high up in the stone tower of the chateau.

Sean was awoken from a deep sleep by the clamour of excited voices in the yard below his bedroom. From his window he saw two men whooping, yelling and swearing as they embraced each other in a wild crazy war dance of delight. The canaries in the aviary flew against the chicken wire in great alarm and Sandy jumped up and down on his short legs barking furiously. Minutes earlier the two men, one a dreamer of dreams and the other a custodian of Empire saw the familiar outline of the pigeon winging towards the town from the Mourne mountains in the south-east. The bird made a languid sortie around the clock spire, then like a lone spitfire approaching the white cliffs of Dover, it performed a graceful loop the loop and, turning in a wide sweeping arc, it glided down towards the safety of the landing strip. Its battle over the exhausted bird taxied into the loft and into the waiting hands of Sean's father, who quickly removed the rubber ring for its leg, placed it in a cartridge which dropped into the clock, and

Above the Clouds

the exact time of 10:44:42 was punched on the paper dial. They knew it was one of the fastest times recorded for many a year.

Then the clock in St Anne's church tower struck eleven and Sean heard from his bedroom the faint notes of the trumpeter at the cenotaph playing the last post, before a great silence enveloped the world.

"They shall not grow old as we who are left grow old, age shall not weary them nor the years condemn, at the going down of the sun and in the morning we shall remember them."
Minutes later, in a voice hoarse with emotion Sean's father shouted to his son, "Come down the stairs will ye, now!".
The young man bounded into the kitchen to be confronted by two ashen faced men.
"Did you notice anything unusual when you brought Herbie down his tea?" demanded his agitated father.
"Please tell me you know where it is. That it's just a joke!" croaked a shaking Herbie.
"What the hell's up?" parried Sean.
"Herbie's loaded service revolver is missing, that's what's up!" said the man from nowhere.
"Where in God's name could it be?" wailed Herbie, his hands flailing the air around him.
"I'm finished in the force if it doesn't turn up", and added, "tell me son, that you took it for a joke when you saw me with my eyes closed."
"I swear to Christ, Herbie I never even saw the gun", answered Sean feebly.
"I never noticed it gone, what with all the excitement with the pigeon, till a couple of minutes ago", lamented the stricken ex-soldier.
Suddenly he grabbed Sean by the shoulders and shouted, "Will you swear on the holy bible that you know nothing about the disappearance of my revolver?" "Now wait a wee minute", interjected Sean's father, who up until that moment had remained impassive even incredulous at this turn of events.
"There's no need for you to accuse a son of mine of stealing the damn gun."
"For God's sake", said Sean, "will both of you calm down. Let's go back down the yard and have another search for it. It can't be far away."
But their search was fruitless. Suddenly Herbie said, "What about that wee Marxist fella that works for you?" "You mean Charlie", replied Sean's father, "he's little more than an armchair socialist, if you ask me."
"That's what you think", replied Herbie. "He's the boyo who's been painting the blue flags on gable walls all round the town. We've been keeping an eye on him for a while now."
"It can't be much of an eye or you'd have caught him red-handed by now", muttered Sean to himself.
"Why didn't I think of him before now?", exclaimed Sean's father, adding, "I told him to unload the empty crates before he went home. Let's go to his house and maybe he can shed some light on the situation."

Above the Clouds

Sean feared the worst by the look on his father's face as he entered the kitchen. "Herbie and I called at Charlie's but there's no sign of him", he said flopping down on the settee and pushing his cap back on his forehead.
"His mother claims she hasn't seen sight nor sound of him and what's left of his fry is still in the oven."

There was a long silence before the father spoke again to his son.
"Do you think he took the gun? You and he are good friends." "I don't know", replied Sean, "but I can tell you that I had absolutely nothing to do with it." "I hope not son", said the sad father, his day of triumph ruined. "If Herbie reports the loss of the gun it will only be a matter of time before both of us will be interrogated by the police."

Sean climbed the stairs to his bedroom, threw himself on the bed, stared at the sky blue ceiling and thought of Eleanor the girl with the far away eyes who was marching to Jerusalem.
Within the hour a widespread manhunt was underway for Charlie, now a fugitive of the Crown. The Donaghmore Road was sealed off by police land-rovers parked nose to tail at either end, and all the houses in between were searched by a baton wielding constabulary. Known republicans were taken from their homes and escorted to the barracks in the square for questioning, but the father and son who lived at number thirty eight Scotch Street were spared the indignity of an official visit for the moment.
Just as it was getting dark Sean slipped on his overcoat and stepped into the street. He walked quickly up a deserted Beechvalley and out on to the Black Lough Road for he was desperate to get out from under the skin of the town. A full moon threw a silvery wash down the slope of the road by O'Brien's hill splashing the dark silhouette of a lone woman with a milky light.
"Look at the moon", Mary said to the approaching Sean.
"It's empty", came the reply.

The both stood still for a moment facing each other and without a further word they began kissing urgently and violently. The lovers' tore and ripped at each other in a silent magnificent frenzy among mingled odours of mouldy hay and cow manure. Then Mary laughed and stroking Sean's tangled hair, said, "You're a right stallion you are", and in the same breath added, "I need you to do me a wee favour, darling."
"Are you on the milk round in the morning?" "I am", said Sean, "for it's a school holiday", and before he could elaborate Mary kissed him on the lips and said, "It will be dark but don't leave the milk on the front step. The side door into the kitchen will be on the latch and I'll be waiting for you there."
Mary gave him a long lingering kiss on the nape of his neck, and whispering in his ear said, "There's a small something I want you to keep for me. It'll only be for a couple of weeks or so until things quieten down around here."

Above the Clouds

"I don't know about that", stammered the youth and stepped back.

Then the hammer blow fell.

"You wouldn't want our little affair to reach the ears of your family or friends now would you?" asked Mary in a voice that rasped like a saw on a rusty nail. In the darkness Sean felt sick, lonely and stricken.

"What is it you want me to keep?" he squeaked like a terrified mouse.

"Never you mind your pretty little head", said the beautiful blackmailer.

Sean's head sort of snapped to one side in an involuntary jerk as if he had been slapped hard across the face, and for some reason he thought of the hapless French knights at Agincourt as the arrows of death rained down on them from the long bows of the English soldiers.

As Mary turned to go she said, "and leave us a couple of extra pints, like a good lad, will ye!" and gave him an outrageous wink.

As the young man stood there everything around him began to move and he felt like he was perched precariously on the side of a giant spinning top. He found it hard to stand upright and lent forward to prevent himself from sliding off the edge of the western world into a vast ocean. Steadying himself by gripping onto a wooden fence post and looking down he saw below him the huge waves that threatened to drown him like the unfortunate wretches in Turner's great watercolour 'The Shipwreck'.

Sean felt suffocated and began to choke and cough. He wretched trails of an orangy vomit down into the salty sea, but the foul smell of seaweed which filled his nostrils forced his head back from the abyss with a sickening jolt. Blinking and spluttering at the same time he wiped his mouth and eyes with the back of his hand in an effort to regain his composure and his senses.

The clanking noise of the couplings on an empty goods wagon as it slowly reversed along the polished tracks caught the attention of the homeward bound lover. He stopped and looked over the parapet of the metal bridge above the tracks laid on countless oily oak sleepers as a black steam engine with the letters N.R. and the numerals 2 and 4 stencilled on white on the side of the cab, shunted the solitary wagon past the rusticated stone outline of the station and its attached two-storey signal box.

During the day the noises and the smells of the town spun themselves into a loose spidery web of invisible threads which attached themselves to lamp-posts, iron railings, chimney pots, walls and crevices like the climbing ivy which covered the station walls in a glorious profusion of bottle green. The song of a caged goldfinch in Harry McRory's hallway in William Street filled the morning air with its music, halted momentarily by the squealing of pigs being butchered in O'Brien's yard nearby. For many a shopkeeper the eight o'clock hooter from Dickson's factory marked the start of their working day, and ten hours later the ringing of the angelus bell high up in the spire of St. Patrick's church marked its close.

Barrels of salted herrings outside McCool's shop in Irish Street smelt of the sea, and from the door of Miss McCrory's further up the street came the whiff of cigars and 'Warhorse' plug

Above the Clouds

tobacco. On a Tuesday evening cow manure washed down the concrete slope of the market yard wafted into the saloon bar of Quinn's public house opposite and mingled with the odour of boiled cabbage from McCooey's eating house a few doors down. From the interior of Dynes' barber shop in Church Street stepped clean shaven men smelling of brylcream and shaving lather who walked down Scotch Street to have their shoes soled and heeled with oiled leather cut from hides hanging by bailer twine in Feeney's chaotic cobblers shop.

5

Sean lay on the bed his arms and legs outstretched and drew an imaginary white line around his body like he had seen the cops doing in American crime movies. Then he drew another line, this time in the shifting sands of an ancient desert kingdom, around 'the vast and trunkless legs of stone' that once supported the huge body of King Ozymandius.

He looked around the room as if he was seeing it for the first time or maybe for the last time and observed its walls, furniture and contents. His eyes darted from the pink wallpaper motifs to the smooth round handles of the chest of drawers, and up to the dusty wings of the model aeroplane, then down to the pile of boxing magazines on the bed opposite.

But every time he blinked his eyes the shining image of Mary appeared like a Lourdes apparition and a throbbing pain not unlike that of a gumboil swept through his groin. He realised how Jesus must have felt when the vinegary spears of the Roman centurions pierced his side as he hung on the Cross at Calvary.

He shut his eyes again but this time he saw a painting of the Crucifixion hanging on a wall in the high ceilinged reception room of the Convent of Mercy, which he had visited as a child along with his mother. His great-aunt Mother Aloysious and some other nuns would fuss around him and his brother, their hand pinching, pressing and caressing their little bodies.

"And which of you young men would like to be a priest when you grow up?", enquired Mother Oliver, her hairy chin inches away from the heads of the startled twins.

The slam of the front door followed by a yelling down in the canyon of the hallway below made Sean sit up with a start. It was the kind of commotion that might have greeted a dust covered pony express rider complete with handle-bar moustache, red bandana, buckskin jacket and colt 45 six gun as he dismounted from an exhausted horse at the end of a wild gallop across the New Mexico badlands.

The excited voice of Herbie Johnston boomed up the hall, "John, John, somebody's been praying for me. I'm a happy this day, so I am."

"What the hell's up with you, Herbie?", his fathers quizzing voice replied.

Dancing around like the great Sioux Chief Sitting Bull doing an Irish jig, Herbie roared, "The gun's been found! I'm saved, thank God Almighty. I'm saved!"

The sound of his voice and the stamping of his boots in the confined space of the hall resonated around and up the spiralling stairs toward the apprehensive young man who stood framed in the open doorway of his bedroom.

Above the Clouds

Sean swayed a little, his hands gripping the jams on either side as if to steady himself. Then he heard his father say, "That's great news", followed by "What you need is a wee glass of Powers", as both men disappeared into the inner sanctum of the living room. In the few seconds that it took Sean to descend the stairs and stride into the parlour he had managed to compose himself sufficiently to exclaim with mock bravado, "What's all the racket about, will ye tell me? You look like a man who's just won the pools, Herbie!"

"Herbie's a relieved man, that's what", said his father, a whiskey bottle in his hand.
Herbie had stuffed his massive bulk into an old armchair with loose side covers that had belonged to his grandmother, and taking off his spectacles with his left hand he wiped his face with the paw of the other, saying, "Bloody relieved is right, John", and turning his head in the direction of Sean, continued, "We've located my revolver, you'll be glad to hear, young fella".

At that he gave the student, who waited in vain for a few seconds to hear all the details, a strange unfocused sort of look. Unnerved, Sean heard himself saying, "That's great news Herbie".

Then the reserve policeman gulped down the entire contents of a brimming glass of whiskey proffered to him in a single childish swallow before Sean's father had time to place a small jug of water on the piano stool beside the armchair.

"You'll need a refill", said the father, without a trace of sarcasm in his voice, as he lifted the empty glass towards the bottle of amber spirits on the mantelpiece above the tiled fireplace.

Sean thought of the baul Stevie Bloomfield and the frosted window of Cush's office in lower Scotch Street. Painted in a perfect arc on the glass were the words P.J. CUSH LLB & CO. LTD in black and gold scripted lettering. Below it the faltering outline of the letters SOLI were partially completed. McKee's public house next door was too much of a distraction for a signwriter who quoted Socrates.

His glasses firmly back on the bridge of his nose, Herbie intoned, "That wee Communist boyo wasn't so smart afterall! It's just as well he skipped over the border for there's no telling what damage a fella like that would do. He was nothing only a bad influence on all around him, if you ask me."

At this salvo the father gave his son an anxious glance but the young admirer of the Bolshevik Revolutionaries was finding the red and blue pattern on the carpet at his feet of particular interest.

"You may as well take a bottle of stout along with the whiskey", said the father, standing up and turning opened the door to the kitchen, where in the back scullery he always kept a couple of bottles on the floor behind the greyhound trays.

Above the Clouds

When he had gone, Herbie leant forward in the armchair of his grandmother's chair and said to Sean, "The boys in the barracks had your friend Charlie under observation for a while now, so they had. Himself and a couple of his cronies were meeting regularly up by O'Brien's hill hear the lough."

At this revelation Sean's heart leapt and he could feel the blood draining from his face, but he daringly looked into Herbie's eyes for some flicker of hidden knowledge or even telepathic communication.

"Tell Sean about the gun", said the father on re-entering the room and handing Herbie a glass of stout.

"Aye, the gun", repeated Herbie slowly, then picking up the pace of his words continued, "That was a bit of a turn up for the books, alright." He paused, and before he spoke again Sean watched as his tongue moistened his fleshy lips, as if he was relishing the words to come.

"One of the Republicans, "the boys", were keeping a close eye on, was a woman, and a bit of a looker too, I'm told".

Herbie sort of smiled to himself as the novelty of it. Sean remained impassive and mute for he was incapable of uttering a single syllable.

"Anyway", continued Herbie, lifting the glass of stout to his lips, then lowering it again to gaze into its frothy head as if he realised the drama of the moment and wanted to prolong it, "her house was raided not an hour ago".

Sean gulped hard as Herbie drank from the glass leaving a foamy line along his bushy moustache, like a high watermark on Portstewart Strand.

"You'll never guess what house it was", interrupted the father turning to Sean, then answering the question himself.

"It was 35 Braeside Close, so it was", and then added, "where your woman Mary McCarthy lives!" "My God", mumbled a shocked Sean.

"I always knew there was something about her", the Nationalist father mused.

"She's a flashy piece of goods alright, I'll give you that", he nodded in the direction of the satisfied ex-soldier who had drained the remainder of the stout from the glass.

Sean sat himself down on the side arm of the family sofa largely to prevent himself from lurching forward so shaken was he by this revelation.

"Are you alright there?" asked Herbie, his massive mitten of a hand gripping the arm of the swaying lover.

"You look a bit pale of yourself, so you do".

"You weren't on the beer last night by any chance?" he added.

The father gave both Herbie and Sean a dark look, and said, "The lad doesn't take a drink, and added, "He can do what he likes in that department after his 21st birthday. That will be up to him."

Above the Clouds

This was indeed true, and although Sean was a 'pioneer' he would have given anything at that moment to be holding a large whiskey in both hands, so scared was he.

Herbie waited a couple of seconds until he was the centre of attention again, "It didn't take long to find the gun. It was lying wrapped in a child's sock, if you don't mind, in the kitchen cupboard. Then he added pityingly, "The Republicans have the women doing their dirty work for them now".

Herbie, it seemed to Sean sounded as if he was coming to the end of a bedtime story, but to his horror another unscripted chapter was added.

He suddenly prized himself from the armchair and began throwing his arms about the room. With spittle flying from his open mouth he began wrestling with himself in an apparent re-enactment of Mary's arrest, saying, "She struggled with three policemen, kicking, scratching, biting and screaming all the way to the landrover, and poor Geordie Benson had his uniform ripped and got a kick in the balls for his trouble!".

As Herbie spun around to demonstrate, his boot knocked over the piano stool, spilling water from the jug over the well-worn carpet. Ignoring it he roared, "and the fucking language of the bitch was a total disgrace, so it was!"

With that he turned triumphantly towards the hall door and in a calmer, steadier voice said, "Well boys, it's time I was off".

As Herbie made his exit from the parlour the defender of the crown rapped his knuckles on his forehead as if to remind himself of something important.

"Oh, I almost forgot," he said, and continued, "She kept screaming, "Who's the bloody informer? Who is he? Who is it?"

Sean remained seated and as his father led Herbie into the gloom of the hallway he heard him say, "We'll be in touch".

About midnight a sleepless young man stood under a full moon in a field below a red shed and gazed into the middle distance. A shield of beaten silver covered the lough as it lay resplendent in the rough fields east of O'Brien's hill, and Sean, shuffling his feet in the damp green scrub sensed the furrowed lines of a plough beneath him.

A Dutch Auction

1

'Lot number twenty seven – one black kettle,' pronounced the auctioneer, standing on the upturned apple box and motioning at the same time to a muscular assistant with the tattooed letters LOVE darkly visible on the fingers of his hairy left hand.

'Hold it up Joe, let these folks have a good look,' he continued.
'Who'll give me five bob, three shillings, two shillings? 'All right then, somebody start me at one and six.'

The auctioneers words hung in the air for a few seconds as he scanned the faces of the small crowd of fidgety neighbours, curious town folk and perennial bargain hunters who stood outside the house of the late Billy Montgomery.

In the obituary column of the local newspaper, 'The Tyrone Courier,' it was noted that, "he had been in indifferent health for some time," and also that 'he had fought with the Inniskilling Fusiliers during World War II, seeing active service in North Africa and Italy."

Sean, who had never been to an auction had struck up a friendship with Billy some months before, for the ex-soldier had often passed the boy as they both wandered the hilly streets that constituted the town proper. Sean was initially surprised when this stranger, a widower and a Protestant had said 'hello' to him in a friendly voice one afternoon in July.

As Sean, a lanky awkward boy stood outside the door of Hamilton's grocery store in Scotch Street, Billy a small bandy-legged man smiled at him and said, 'I saw you the other day down in Conway's field by the lough.' The bony teenager replied, 'I heard a couple of goldfinches singing from the top of the road so I went looking for them, but they flew out of a thorn bush before I could get next or near them.'

Since the start of the summer holidays Sean had spent many hours exploring the sprawling hilly fields, lush meadows and thick fruity hedgerows that surrounded the Black Lough, which lay glistening on the western flank of the town. Unusually for the time he was an only child but not a lonely one.

'I've got a couple of goldfinches in box cages at home, so I have, and you're welcome to call at any time to see them,' said the birdman, 'Thanks, that's great,' said Sean shyly.

During the rest of the summer months the wee war veteran and the gangly youth were often seen knee deep in the rushy green fields that sloped gently down to the edge of the lough. They

A Dutch Auction

also tramped the lowlands of Killabrackey and the burning sands of Mulbuoy in their quest for speckled eggs, jellied frogspawn and of course the retreating Axis forces of the Afrika Korps under the command of 'the desert fox,' field marshal Erwin Rommel. Billy would often drop on one knee among the swaying foxgloves, thistles and burdock and point his walking stick in the direction of a fresian heifer its legs ankle deep in muddy shoreline water, as if he was a soldier aiming his rifle at a German paratrooper. In reality Billy confessed that he had never shot anyone and being small had spent most of his time carrying ammunition, peeling potatoes or running errands for his company sergeant – major.

'One and six, then, one and six – it's for nothing!' intoned the auctioneer, his eyes darting in and out of the faces before him, for some flicker of interest.

'Good man yourself,' he said, nodding in the direction of a ginger haired fellow dressed in dungarees and Wellington boots standing by an apple tree in the middle of a neat garden edged with a low privot hedge.

'Anyone else? It has to be sold, everything has to go there's no reserve?, he barked.

A female voice at the front said hesitatingly, 'Two bob,' 'That's more like it,' said the auctioneer, valuator and undertaker, and added smiling, 'Its scalded many's the ass off a pig in its time.'
Then looking down at the timid woman he said with an air of triumph, 'The kettles' yours ma'am for the princely sum of two shillings.'
Turning to his assistant he scowled and muttered, 'Keep her lit Joe – next lot – hold it up, let the dogs see the hare.'
The stocky middle-aged auctioneer in the crumpled suit who stood outside the semi-detached orlit bungalow at number seven Lakeside Villas on the Saturday after Billy's sudden death read aloud from a typed sheet of paper,'Lot number twenty eight – a wire bird-cage.'
Sean watched as the empty cage was held aloft and thirty seconds later it was 'knocked down' to a tall man with a roman nose for five shillings. Billy knew all the collective nouns for birds – a charm of goldfinches, a clamour of rooks, a cast of hawks, a fall of woodcock, a host of sparrows, a muster of peacocks, a paddling of ducks, a whisp of snipe, a watch of nightingales and most glorious of all, an exultation of larks.
Billy's council house was in the middle of a cluster of twelve 'pre-fabs' built by the government after the war as part of an unexpected or unforeseen housing crisis. Though hardly 'homes fit for heroes' these standard issue formula-built bungalows with their asbestos roof slates and identical end-porches were sturdy comfortable houses.
For the next hour or so Kenny Smyth the auctioneer rattled off a list of assorted items, the entire possessions of an old soldier who had never hurt anyone. Three blackthorn sticks, a

A Dutch Auction

mantel clock, two shell cases, and orange sash, small table, suitcase, box of cutlery, world war two medals, box of miscellaneous items, wall mirror, brass fire irons, tilley lamp, garden shears, spade, chamber pot, old bible .....

Methodically and expertly the crumply man stripped the house of its contents with all the skill of a monkey peeling a banana until there was no trace left of Billy Montgomery. Sean was disturbed by this state of affairs but not for long – for he was hungry. So he turned and headed back towards the spikey spires of the town along the Eglish Road that skirted the eastern side of the lough. Earlier that afternoon he had walked out the mile and a half or so from his home near the town centre, along the higher Black's Road on the lough's western side.

As the empty road turned to meet a scattering of new red brick houses that belonged to business men, shop owners and civil servants Sean moved smartly to its cambred centre and with arms swinging forward and backwards he marched along whistling 'It's a long way to Tipperary.' From deep in a thicket came the accompanying song of a goldfinch and turning his head he spotted its splendid yellow and red plumage among the green and olive foliage.

Some day I might be a soldier, he speculated, thinking of the Irish Guards, who, resplendent in red and black uniforms, their ceremonial bear-skin busbys secured with silver chin straps, had beaten retreat the Saturday before in the town square. And out from the pages of history marched the Irish Brigade, the 'wild geese' who fought with distinction under Marshal Tallard at the battle of Blenheim in 1704. Another battle, unknown to him was about to unfold in a desert kingdom split in half by the Suez canal.

At a fork in the road he slackened his pace and turned right towards Carson's hill and the drop down into Beechvalley, and as he felt the rise of the gradient he slowed to a leisurely gait. Strange new words filled his mouth and spilled like stones from a labourers shovel into a hole in the road as he struggled to smooth them down into a rough surface of understanding. He attempted to exchange the nouns which surrounded him with the ancient Latin and Irish ones that he had come across in school lessons.

The word in Irish for 'field' was 'gort,' the word for 'hill' he couldn't remember, but the townland name 'Annaghbeg' he thought meant 'the small marsh,' with the adjective coming after the noun. In Latin the word for 'farmer' was 'agricula' and it pleased him that the name had found its way down the centuries into common usage. 'urbs, urbis,' he knew was the singular and plural for a 'city,' but the name for a 'town' escaped and perplexed him.

It had taken the boy soldier about twenty minutes to reach the outer ramparts of the great metropolis. As he crossed over the drawbridge to the sanctuary within he fingered the coins in his right trouser pocket and headed straight for Mac's fish and chip saloon at the junction of Irish Street and Ann Street.

'Give us a double meat-roll please,' said Sean to a small black-haired woman with close set eyes, pale complexion and pinched nostrils.

A Dutch Auction

'Salt and vinegar?' asked Elsie O'Neill in a matter of fact sort of way as she turned towards the cauldron behind her which seethed and bubbled with frying chips and battered portions of white fish. Sean didn't answer for Elsie was already pouring salt into a white paper bag dripping with the hot fat from the crispy battered rolls of mince meat propped there along with a couple of chips. If she was in a good mood Elsie would half-fill the wee bag with chips, but not today. 'That's sixpence to you,' she said dryly, dropping the bag into a larger brown one and then deftly spinning it round in a twist with both hands before skidding it across the red formica covered counter.

The chip shop was packed with customers many of whom sat at large communal tables covered with a plastic laminate and edged with an aluminium border inset with a thin black strip. The menu, which never varied was written in chalk on a black-board which advertised coca-cola and was attached to the wall between two large windows. It read, fish and chips, single fish, single chip, sausage supper, meat roll, meat roll supper, cup of tea, glass of milk, orange mineral or coke. The soft drinks came in the bottle complete with straw.

Sean handed the sixpence to Miss O'Neill and lifting the bag from the counter turned for the door.

'Well young fella how's your da these days?' said the voice of Eddie Tracey who was sitting alone at a small table near the exit.
'He's all right as far as I know,' said the boy and as he paused the man roughly grabbed the pocket of his jacket and pulled him forward over the table.

'Your father always helped me out if I was down on me luck' he said, his face inches from that of Sean's nose. The smell of stale beer that wafted up his nose made the boy wince, as he placed his free hand on the table top to prevent himself from pitching forward and scattering the plate of chips that sat untouched beside the vinegar jar and the white capped salt cellar. Eddie let go of the jacket and slumped back on his chair breathing heavily like a boxer on his stool near the end of a hard fight. Then looking up into the brightness beyond the outline of the youth he shouted, 'Where's the glass of milk I ordered. Is there anybody going to serve a poor soul like myself?'

Eddie had returned from England a month or so before to bury his father, after a lifetime of navvying on a variety of building sites and road construction works in the Midlands around Manchester. His hands were heavy, tanned and thick and he had the look of a man who worked hard and drank harder. He had in fact spent most of his time since the funeral in quite a few of the thirty odd public houses that the town boasted, and stories about his exploits had curled like lashes around the place of his birth. It was said that he had masterminded a famous jewel robbery while others claimed that he had been bigamously married to the daughter of an English lord.

A Dutch Auction

An old scar ran across his left cheek bone and over the bridge of his nose, and his eyes were fringed with egg yellow shading to red along the lids. Eddie's lips were swollen and cracked, and from a small gash high up on his forehead trickled a meandering line of blood that congealed along the arch of his greying eyebrow. To Sean, he looked like the battered face of Rinty Monaghan on the night he became Ireland's first world boxing champion by knocking out the durable Scot Jackie Paterson in Belfast.

Sean straightened up as Eddie said in a confidential whisper, 'Lend me a few bob, will ye?', adding 'Things aren't going so well for me right now.'

Cruelly the youth replied, 'What do you mean, 'lend me a few bob?' why, am I going to get it back? Don't you mean, give me a few bob!' Eddie just shrugged his shoulders at this hurtful and uncharitable repost, and as Sean disappeared out of the door he lifted a chip with his fingers and placed it abstractly in his mouth.

Sean ate the double 'hot-dog' and chips with some relish as he walked up Irish Street past McAnespie's confectionary shop where he occasionally bought a flaky cream bun and two woodbine cigarettes for the same price as the 'hot-dogs.' Turning into Shamble lane he almost collided with Billy Whitmore who was coming out of McQuaide's bookies shop.

'Oh, terribly sorry old chap.' muttered Billy apologetically, adding 'dirty old day,' even though the afternoon was warm and dry, Billy was a 'runner' for Mulgrew's public house in Scotch Street and always included in every conversation the same phrase. His life revolved around the pub, and in the mornings he would tidy up, cross the road for the newspapers and cigarettes from Quinn's shop opposite, run errands and in the afternoon place bets for the patrons. He did all this in exchange for a couple of bottles of free stout and the odd glass of whiskey. Knitting his eyebrows anxiously this thin man of tidy appearance who always wore a clean shirt and tie said in a voice that suggested an imminent tussle with destiny, 'Must dash, you know, things to do,' and scampered away.

'Toucher' Deane, who had a nose the size and colour of an over-ripe plum patronised Stewarts pub up Irish Street, 'Wanker' Hughes, with brylcreamed hair and shirt open to the waist in all weathers hung around Packie Quinn's in lower Scotch Street. McKee's pub, a couple of doors down was the haunt of Norrie 'how's your mother' Forsyth and Paddy 'the wack' Loughlin who was a permanent feature around Loy's pub in Ann Street was always accompanied by frisky lurcher pups.

As the dusty rickety shadows of the lane's buildings swept the narrow roadway with diagonal brush-strokes of the deepest grey, an alert mongrel terrier darted out of a dim hallway and snatched the empty chip bag which Sean had thrown down at his heels. He aimed a flying kick at the speeding dog as if he intended to kick a hole in the world but the crafty animal swerved away and ran off down Sloan Street. Old Mrs Duggan watched without interest from behind her lace curtains.

A Dutch Auction

2

The town's rooftops of broken Bangor slates, walls of crumbling masonry, cracked chimneys and exposed weather-beaten bricks the colour of burnt copper and deepest vermilion gave it an air of defeat. It did however boast a few buildings which were distinguished from the chaotic clutter of small shops and dwellings that lined the streets by their impressive presence, unusual design or sheer size.

One such building was St Patrick's church, known as 'the chapel' which stood at the junction of Northland Row and Killyman Road. During the long summer days when not criss-crossing the vast drumlin landscape that sprawled for ever beyond the craggy roofs of the town Sean was drawn like a moth to a flame, into its stony embrace.

With his eyes the boy builder followed the thrust of its incised and splendidly carved spire all the way upwards until the cross of its vanishing point split the sky in two equal halfs some two hundred feet above, and in the afternoon sunshine it glittered like a diamond in a shale mountain.

Sean often walked around the perimeter walls of the chapel always in a clockwise direction, his left hand lightly tracing his fingers along the ashlar squared blocks of sand stone quarried from nearby Carland, Gortnaglush and Bloomhill. Sometimes he pressed his index finger on to the bluff chiselled stone like a child feeling and groping at its mother's face and neck, but all he experienced was the hard sandpapery roughness of its cold unyielding surface.

He was still unaware of the thousands of pilgrims who had down the years humbled themselves in prayer and penance by trudging around holy places like Lough Derg, Lourdes or Fatima. In his journey of discovery Sean, like Magellan or Amerigo Vespucci, just travelled westwards in hope and with few navigational aids to guide him. But by counting each stone in his longitudinal journey and marking each prominent feature he soon charted a course in his mind that gave him a rudimentary sense of the scale, proportion and volume of this great landmass of a church.

Initially all he had to go on was a small wall plaque just inside the side entrance above the holy water font which stated, "St Patrick's' Church, designed by architects' J.J. and C.T. McCarthy was erected in 1876, the tower and spire being completed in 1889." No mention was made of the bowler-hatted stone masons or the other artisans who had toiled for years over its exquisite construction. No mention either of the towns' strongest men who vied with one another for the honour of hoisting the three and half ton bell on to a four-wheeled wagon at

A Dutch Auction

the railway station in Beechvalley, just arrived from the Dublin iron foundry of J. Murphy, and then pulling it like Egyptian slaves all the way to its final destination.

Soon the boy could tell the exact time of day by the stealthy advance of the hard edged shadow as it crept over the unsuspecting grass lawn that sloped down to the boundary wall along the chapel's western side. As the cold finger of the spire touched the warm stone flags on the first step down to the sexton's house the town clock struck four.

Sometimes Sean pressed both hands against its massive flank and looked skywards until his head began to spin and his bony frame shudder. The dark boughs of the nearby Scotch pine trees creaked in a freshening breeze and unsettled the quarrelsome crows who flew in and out of the branches cawing their disapproval.

Opposite his home in Scotch Street the library service had rented rooms above George McCrea's drapery shop, and here he had seen photographs in history books of the magnificent cathedrals of the thirteenth and fourteenth centuries such as Cantebury, Chartres and Cologne.

The historians had all claimed that "they represented the pinnacle of Gothic ecclesiastical architecture." This puzzled the young reader who had yet to discover that his chapel was in reality a nineteenth century facsimile and was part of a cultural phenomenon known as Gothic revivalism. When the revelation that McCarthy had copied an earlier style dawned on him he felt as if his head was full of glass. For an architect to look backwards over the shoulder of history was he felt questionable and as his eyes fell on a photograph of the pyramids he felt certain that no one would be so foolish as to attempt to build a modern copy of this icon.

Now he realised that St Patrick's was first and foremost a Roman church, a Latin-church, and as such part and parcel of a religious empire that flourished like the 'ivy hibernicus' that grew up and over the old ramparts of O'Neill's castle in a glorious steely profusion, until in time stone and vine became one and indivisible. The stone blocks, carefully chiselled and laid, course upon course by Irish hands, gradually formed themselves into a cultural cocoon of immense size and weight. Perhaps, though Sean, this was its secret and its flaw – to be born old and venerable.

On the warmest of summer days the interior of the chapel was always splendidly cool and still, and Sean would sit in different pews and just look around him. Once he lay flat out on a pine bench about half way up the hundred foot long central aisle, and staring at the hammer-beam vaulted ceiling counted twenty four arched beams that supported the roof coupling of wooden panels and ribs.

Other times he would watch the soft shafts of sunlight that filtered through the coloured quatrefoils in the rose window blend with the sharper paler light that radiated down from the thin lancet windows into a tinted mothy glow. Down near the floor tiles millions of dust particles danced energetically before the gathering gloom stole the light. He would often stand in front of the tongue-tied statues of St Theresa and St Anthony sensing that behind their blank masks they longed for the comfort of a warm overcoat and a woolly scarf.

The boy and his parents always attended a packed chapel on Sunday's for the twelve-thirty mass, and after the final blessing by the priest the congregation spilled out along Northland

A Dutch Auction

Row, like the match-stick men in a L.S. Lowry painting. He watched the older woman smiling benevolently at each other secure in the knowledge that their faith entitled them at the close of their lives to the beatific vision, the heavenly kingdom that lay somewhere above the snowy Himalayan mountain range in distant Nepal.

Fellows like Jackie Bartley and Joey McCann who stood at the back of the chapel and talked about football throughout the mass might, on the other hand have a more difficult time squeezing through the pearly ice gates. Aside from the Sunday masses, early week-day masses, funerals, weddings and christenings were all performed with a perfunctory regularity.

Masses require altar boys, lots of them and Sean found himself part of a team known as the 'Scotch Street brigade' simply because they all lived in the same street. Their job was to serve the early week-day masses at seven thirty and eight o'clock for a couple of weeks several times a year.

The group which consisted of five boys including Sean, were the Corr brothers Jim and Frankie, and Michael and Patrick Kelly. The Corrs lived at the top of the street on the opposite side and their father who was a taxi driver spent most of his time ferrying priests and nuns to churches and convents or to the houses of the hapless, the bereaved or the destitute of the parish.

On the same side of the street but a few doors down lived the Kelly's, a family of four boys and two girls. As they lived about Lewis's butcher shop they had no front door but access was gained through a side door half way up a narrow grey entry. Mickey who was the eldest, was known as 'scrawa' and had a sallow complexion, deep set eyes and enormous ears. Because he was the eldest he took it upon himself to act as team leader, which included swearing at everyone particularly his brother, and threatening to 'cut the balls off' anyone who didn't serve the mass properly.

Sean would kneel on the bottom step of the marble altar and watch the priest moving along its length performing a ritual that seemed as constant and as ancient as the North star. The Latin words he spoke never varied, nor did his own responses that he didn't really understand but recited mechanically. The repetitive resonance of the word sounds, like the beating of his heart echoed down the centuries, past the famine, past the battle of Clontarf and all the way to the hill of Tara. Here in his own town the vernacular threads of this archaic language still lingered in the damp laneways for he knew that a monastery filled with monks had once lived and prayed on the site of the gasworks at Washingford row. These scribes, he surmised wrote letters on vellum to their superiors in Reims or Rome in the first universal language of an awakening world.

As the priest raised the host aloft at the consecration Sean struck the brass gong with a small round mallet and watched him move to the right side of the altar to have wine and water poured into a gold chalice. Then the eyes of the kneeling boy were instinctively drawn to the life-size carving of the dead figure of Christ lying horizontally in a rebated inset below the altar table; a tragic marble figure that pined for his Palestinean homeland.

A Dutch Auction

'Caide mara ta tu, a hSean óg?' said the sacristan as the altar boy pushed the heavy vestry door shut with his scrawny behind.
'I'm alright,' answered Sean to Mark McCool, the sacristan and fervent Gaelic Leaguer, who acknowledged the slight with the faintest hint of a smile. The air was heavy with the sweet and pungent mixture of incense, candle wax and moth balls as he buttoned a red soutane over the top of his shirt and jumper.

The sacristan, a small middle-aged man who walked with a pronounced limp always spoke in Irish to anyone with even a smattering of the Gaelic as if this willingness to converse in another tongue was an enobling thing. Of late the boy noticed that his conversations to one priest in particular were always serious and sometimes animated. Once, when unfamiliar syllables spilled from his mouth like jelly off a spoon he stopped open-mouthed and glanced anxiously at the altar boys, as if he was afraid that he may have unwittingly revealed some great secret, but only the urgent song of the words reached their ears.

'Here, take the matches and light the candles,' said Mark to Sean, as Father McMahon strode into the sacristy. Then quietly and reverentially he placed a hand on the boys' shoulder and whispered into his ear, in Irish, 'And get a fucking move on, you little prick.'

A few minutes later as Sean returned from the altar the sacristan and the priest were whispering and nodding to each other in a grim desolate way as if they were passing some great secret back and forward, the weight of which was threatening to cripple both of them. Sean thought of Paddy Hughes the coalman who hawked two one hundred weight bags of coal into his fathers yard every second Tuesday.

The altar servers formed up in a ragged line as Father McMahon placed the heavy green and gold brocaded chasuble over his shoulders. Sean glanced at the sacristan, a servant of God who ruled the Gothic fiefdom from within. This was his prison here on earth and like the umbilical cord that unites mother and child in the womb he was the buckle in the church's belt. It was he who climbed the stone steps above the choir loft to ring the angelus bell every evening, it was he who refilled the carved baptismal font with holy water; it was he who swept the aisles and transepts and polished the brass candelebra, and it was Mark who scraped the splatters of candle wax from the altar cloths.

One afternoon in late August as Sean sat in a side aisle directly opposite a carved oak confessional box a voice behind him said, 'The show doesn't start till six o'clock as far as I know.' The startled boy spun around to see Eddie Tracey sitting in the pew directly behind him, who leaning forward gripped the top of the wooden bench with his ham of a hand and continued, 'You must have a hell of a lot of sins to get off your chest, young fella, if you ask me.'
'No, its its not that,' exclaimed the boy, aware that his voice had betrayed both his fright and his embarrassment at being discovered sitting outside a confessional at five o'clock on a summer evening. His embarrassment deepened when he remembered what he had said to Eddie in Mac's fish and chip shop a few weeks earlier. Sean shifted round in the seat and pointing his index finger up towards the foliated capital of a massive column in fine-tooled block stone, said, 'Do

A Dutch Auction

you see them?' 'See what?' queried Eddie, squinting up at the stone anthemion leaves that spread up and around the cornice.

'Look, there, up there, can you see them now,?' the excited Sean exclaimed, and raising to his feet grabbed the curious Eddie by the shoulder.

'Are you blind or what?' Look up, there's a carved bird and a monkey peeping down!'

'Good Christ,' said Eddie, 'You're right, all right, I can see them now. They're sort of hiding among the leaves. Well fuck me,' He laughed and said 'The bird looks like a pigeon with its wings spread out as if it wants to do a shit, and look at your man with the tail and the cheeky face of him.'

Eddie gave a low reverential whistle that echoed down the empty chapel, and moved to the base of the column to get a better look.

'I only just spotted them a second before you put the frighteners on me,' said Sean, excited by the discovery and glad to share it with someone, anyone.

'Well that a good 'un,' answered the old campaigner, and with his eyes still fixed on the capital said, 'I wonder who it was?' 'Wonder who what was?,' asked Sean, then added, 'Maybe it was a mason who got bored of carving leaves and decided to add something else.'

'Who ever it was, he was pretty good,' answered Eddie.

'Maybe there's more of them on the columns,' said Sean.

Together man and boy examined all eight capitals of the Bloomhill pillars that supported the roof couplings by walking slowly round them, their eyes peering up into the dressed stonework. About an hour later as the light from the lancet windows with their plate tracery dimmed and a gathering gloom crept like a thief along the side aisles and into the transepts, they had found no more evidence of the mason who lifted the spirits of those who chose to look up.

As they left the chapel Eddie crossed himself in a clumsy, abbreviated way and turning to Sean said in a voice that suggested no little regret, 'It's a long time now since I darkened the door of a church but since I've been back I drop in the odd time, and anyway I suppose old habits die hard.'

He paused, adding, 'If it s a wet day this is as good a place as any to pass the time.'

Remarks such as this are hardly doing the reputation of a rambler a gambler and a street-fighter any good at all, thought Sean to himself. At the wrought iron entrance gates Sean said, 'See ye, Eddie,' to which he replied, 'Sure, say maybe you could show me round the place here? Ye seem to know a bit about its history and all that stuff.'

Eddie gave a vague half-smile, and as the boy looked at his tobacco stained teeth, said, 'I'm at a bit of a loose end these days.'

Sean was flattered by the comments from the old warhorse, and readily agreed to act as his unofficial guide.

The young guide had no idea how old Eddie was and guessed he must be about fifty, though looking at his weather beaten face it bore a remarkable resemblance to the rusticated sandstone

A Dutch Auction

of the church walls. His rugged appearance, however, hinted at a man who would have been considered handsome in earlier times. He was small and stocky, and his hair which looked like it had been liberally dusted with talcum powder, was doggedly unruly and curled up playfully around his ears and the nape of his bullish neck.

Over the next few weeks a middle aged man in an ill fitting jacket and baggy trousers accompanied by a bony youth in open-necked shirt and brown sandals were to be seen, like a pair of summer moths, flitting about the environs of St Patrick's, winging their way around the punctuated spaces of the interior and the soaring bulk of the façade, in a busy irreverent journey of discovery

Sean was pleased to tell Eddie what he knew about the history of the church, most of it gleaned from his father, from library books and occasionally from old people who frequently prayed there and volunteered their knowledge.

Eddie looked at the crucified Christ hanging from a large wooden cross and said with a chuckle, 'You're man's took a right hammering, by the looks of him.'

But Sean was puzzled by the fact that the Romans drove the nails through the wrists of their victims to support the dead weight of the body without wrenching it from the cross and not as depicted here, through the palms of the hands.

'I suppose you nailed a few in your time?' he asked.

Without answering the question directly Eddie told Sean of a famous fight he had with the English gypsy Ned Stokes, and how he soaked his face and hands in brine to toughen him up. The fight ended amid pandemonium when he was struck across the bridge of the nose with a broken stout bottle. Eddie managed to recount the story with some dignity in this mausoleum of piety and sobriety and Sean felt envious of a warrior who had wandered the length and breath of England while he had only been to Belfast once, and that was to visit his uncle Seamus, who lived on the Ravenhill Road. Eddie rubbed the white scar on the bridge of his nose, then tapped it knowingly with a finger, saying 'See ye the marra, I've things to do.'

The following afternoon like a latter day Stanley and Livingstone they made a desultory reconnoitre around the foothills of the sacred mountain. Setting up camp opposite the main twin-doored entrance porch they spent some time viewing the figures sculpted in high relief in the tympanium above the door head.

'What's going on up there,?' asked the leader of the expedition.

'That's Saint Patrick on Slemish mountain surrounded by the people of Ireland,' answered his lieutenant.

'Ye don't say,' muttered the leader, adding 'They're a chancey looking bunch. I think we'll press on.'

They broke camp and as they marched on Eddie told Sean about his battles with the booze, and how he often ended up stoney broke on a Monday morning, and worse still unable to lift a shovel on the building site till the afternoon, because of a mighty hangover. He was less

A Dutch Auction

forthcoming however about his romantic exploits with the girls in the shamrock clubs around Manchester, or the stories about his so-called marriage to the daughter of an English lord. Sean was too shy to ask him about the disappearance of the gold chain of office that belonged to the Mayor of Manchester during a gala reception, but rumour had it that Eddie had been the brains behind the scam.
'You shouldn't believe all you hear about me,' said Eddie, winking at the boy and added, 'Just the half of it.'

Suddenly they came to a clearing in the forest, and frowning Eddie walked forward saying, 'Hey, take a look at that writing, there, up on the wall.'
Between the smooth chiselled lines and surfaces of the string courses and directly under a set of thin lancet windows with pointed arches and linked vertical mullions, Sean read aloud a Latin inscription, "Domine, dilexi decorum domus tuae; et locum habitationis gloriae tua."
'What does it say,?' asked Eddie, Sean knew that the question was coming before he had finished speaking, and tried to sound confident as he was unsure of the verb 'delexi,'
'I think it says, "Lord, I have loved the beauty of your house; and the dwelling of your glory."
'Now, what does that mean, in plain English, will ye tell me,? probed Eddie.
'Your guess is as good as mine,' answered the boy translator, but in his mind the message contained in the meticulously carved letters seemed so pompous, and aloof.

They moved on till they came to the last base camp below the summit of the stone obelisk.
'How far is it to the summit,?' gasped the goggled mountaineer.
'About two hundred feet straight up,' answered the sherpa.
'That's still a hell of a way and the weather's turning against us,' said Eddie, as a light shower of rain flecked his coat.
'You go on alone, I'm too old to make it to the top,' he continued and then suddenly tiring of the charade added, 'see you about four tomorrow – if its dry,' and was gone. Sean looked up at the decorated pinnacles and arches that pointed all the way up the symmetrical ice-face of the chapel and decided it was time for him to go home too.

The next afternoon as Sean entered the chapel he heard the raised voice of the sacristan, 'Do you think I haven't noticed ye hanging about this house of God? You're a bit of a light fingered gent by all accounts, I'm told. If I was you I'd take myself out of here right now.'
Sean moved forward silently until he stood behind the 'Balmoral' columns of polished Swedish granite that supported the choir gallery, and saw the figures of the sacristan and Eddie facing one another by the candle-stand near the altar rails.

'Can't I light a candle in memory of my dead parents?' asked Eddie in a quiet respectful voice, and reaching down lifted a white candle from a brass box while at the same time dropping a

A Dutch Auction

coin into the slot at the front of the stand. He lit the candle, placed it in a holder and bowed his head as if in prayer. The sacristan taken aback by this unexpected display of piety and embarrassed at his own lack of composure and foolishness turned away, and disappeared into the dimness of the sanctuary.

'That's the second time in twenty four hours I've been told to clear off,' said Eddie laconically as Sean approached the altar rails.

They both looked at the story of creation depicted in the stained glass rose window with its quatrefoils behind the main altar for a moment or two before he told Sean about his first encounter.

Eddie slept in the back seat of an Austin twelve car that sat outside the home of P.G. McQuaid, a bookmaker who lived at the top of the Donaghmore Road. The bookie had won the car in a poker school in St Patrick's Hall a week before Eddie's return to the town, and as he already had a car he let him doss in it until he found suitable lodgings.

About two o'clock in the morning a platoon of 'B' special police surrounded the car, woke Eddie, and not being satisfied with his answers to their questions they took him to the police barracks in the town square. There he was further questioned and man-handled for several hours before being grudgingly released.

'Away back to England, you tosser,' sneered Mervyn Douglas, the part-time sergeant and hardware store owner, and then as a parting shot roared after Eddie as he crossed the square above the war memorial 'and take those Fenian playboys with you, for they do nothing only hang around the electric board corner all week annoying everyone. All ye are good for is collecting the dole money on a Thursday, and shouting about a united Ireland.'

'You can't go on sleeping in the back of a car,' said Sean anxiously.

'Don't worry about me son,' answered Eddie, and with a grin said, 'I think I've just found somewhere more suitable.'

Then turning he took a step back towards the candle stand, lifted out a couple of candles from the box and stuffed them into an inside pocket of his jacket.

At that moment Sean felt himself bound to the man as though on a see-saw with him, and pinned to an axis that could tip them into each others lives.

A Dutch Auction

3

Sean returned to school in early September and abandoned the still warm fields and the lanes that dissected them, for the compulsory grind of lessons and homework. The walled splendour of the chapel was no longer explored, but visited only on a Sunday for mass, and as for Eddie he just disappeared, like snow off a ditch.

On a cool Saturday afternoon towards the end of the month Sean's father burst into the kitchen of his home where Sean sat at the table wrestling with a page of quadratic equations, with the news of a daring robbery.

'Wait till you hear this,' he said with obvious relish. 'Oul 'soapie' Douglas, up in Church Street was robbed last night as he slept in his own bed. The thief broke in and stole a bundle of notes from the ass pocket of his police trousers.'

The boy laughed at the wonder of it and exclaimed, 'Did he not hear anything?'
'Obviously not,' answered the father and sitting down began to loosen the laces of his working boots. Then he straightened his back and smiling grimly said, 'It couldn't have happened to a better man, the tight-fisted Orange skitter!'

The drama of the robbery and his father's telling of it was not lost on Sean.
'Him and his wife snored like two sows in a pen while the robber lifted the trousers that were hanging by the braces from the bedpost and got the money,' exclaimed the father, and turning round used his finger and thumb in a mock exaggerated gesture to lift imaginary notes from his own back pocket.

'How did he break in?' asked Sean.
'They're saying that who ever it was must have scaled the roof tops of Hamilton's and McQueen's houses and then got in through a small window at the back of the hardware store.

Then he calmly climbed the stairs to their bedroom', said the father, tip toeing across the kitchen floor in his stocking soles as if he was climbing the stairs.

The algebra was forgotten as Sean mused, 'There'll be boys lifted this evening over this, I suppose' 'You suppose right,' he answered and went on, 'but according to 'know all' Benson who works in the store they think it was the work of an expert, a cat burglar.' 'How so they make that out?' asked the student of algebra.

A Dutch Auction

'Well for a start no local would have the stupidity or the balls to steal anything from a policeman, especially a 'B' special, if you ask me,' pondered the father turned detective. Then returning to his chair continued with his revelations and deductions.

'A rubber sink plunger was stuck to a glass pane in the window, and a neat circle cut round it with a glass cutter. All the thief had to do was put his gloved hand inside the hole in the glass and pull up the snib.'

'How do you know all this?' queried Sean.

'Sure it's the talk of the town,' answered his dad saying, 'In any case the plunger was found by the window this morning and beside it was a bit of a candle.'

'A what?' gasped Sean, 'A candle did you say?' 'The wax of the candle deadens the scraping noise of the cutter,' deduced the father, 'and as it was a cloudy night the thief obviously lit the candle for a second or two to see what he was doing,' he concluded and folded his arms with a flourish.

In the third week of November the 'Scotch Street brigade' were back on altar duty. On the Tuesday morning after mass Father McMahon had asked for their help to assemble the Christmas crib and figures at the back of the chapel in preparation for the advent celebrations. After school that afternoon only Sean and Jim Corr presented themselves for voluntary labour at the sacristy door.

The sacristan gave the boys a watery smile with the greeting, 'A caed mile fáilte, roat.'

Sean knew that the plaster Nativity figures of Joseph, Mary, the baby Jesus, the three wise men, two shepherds along with two donkeys and three sheep were stored in St Theresa's hall directly under the western flank of the chapel. They couldn't be anywhere else for the basement hall was the only part that he and Eddie had never explored simply because it was always securely locked.

This last few weeks however, as he passed the chapel on his way to and from the Academy to 'study' from six thirty until nine o'clock, a school requirement for all pupils who lived in the town, he had seen a light coming from a small window near the hall door. Other times he had seen the black outline of figures silhouetted in the open doorway as they left the place, and once several men had brushed past him as they exited through the entrance gates. He knew they were Gaelic Leaguers for they spoke to one another in Irish, and someone had said to him that they were rehearsing a play to be performed at a drama festival in Dundalk town hall, in the new year.

The sexton unlocked the door to St Theresa's hall and stepped into a long low-ceilinged dusty room followed by the boys. Their eyes looked along the line of his pointed finger to a pile of old chairs, some with legs and arms missing, which were haphazardly piled in the middle of the gloomy hall. Just visible behind the wooden stack were the nearly life-size figures of three oriental looking men, one a negro and all in flowing painted robes clutching their presents of gold, frankincense and myrrh.

'Lets get these boys out of here, I have other things to do so I have,' muttered the sexton adding, 'so lets not take all day about it.'

A Dutch Auction

To Sean the pitch of his voice and the way his shoulders moved up and down suggested that he was nervous even alarmed at their presence there among the relics of their faith. He fussed around as they carried and dragged the statues to the open door, pushing and prodding at them like a cattle drover in the market yard on a Tuesday.

'Joe's lost a couple of his fingers,' said Sean to Jim, beads of sweat forming on his brow as they struggled with the inert form of Saint Joseph.
'He'll not do much carpentry now, that's for sure,' replied Jim.
'Get a bloody move on, will ye,' implored Mark, spinning around like a frightened kitten.

In about an hour all the statues had been manhandled out through the door and on to the concrete path below the stone steps that led up to the side entrance of the chapel. At the top of the steps the sacristan motioned the boys to carry up the nearest statue, that of a shepherd and disappeared inside. Seeing that the shepherd's crook was missing from his hand Sean turned back into the hall to look for it.

By now the daylight was fading fast and the interior was in virtual darkness so he switched on the light. A pale yellow glow radiated out from a single bulb suspended from the ceiling like the light from a distant planet. The crook was lying on the floor in the far corner. Pushed against the wall was a sturdy table he hadn't really noticed before and strewn over it were copies of the Legion of Mary magazine, the little Sacred Heart messenger and the Irish language paper An Tultach. As Sean bent down to lift the crook he could see part of a large wooden crate with stencilled letters on its side under the table, and on top if it were folded grey blankets. Lying close to the end leg of the table were the burnt ends of several candles.

Just as the boy, armed with the crook had switched off the light the sacristan lunged at him, half knocking him over and slammed the door shut. In a voice breathless with emotion and no little menace said, 'What do you think you were doing in there?'
'I was only getting the shepherd's stick or whatever its called. Sure without it he looks like a man giving the victory sign,' answered Sean.

The sacristan gave him a disgusted look and with that turned a large key in the lock and then thrust it deep into the pocket of his ample trousers, saying, 'Let's get these statues up into the church before Easter.'

It was dark outside by the time they had finished, when Mark, instead of thanking them turned to Sean with the words, 'Keep you away from here in the future, do ye hear me?'

You've no business poking about this church, it's the house of the Lord and not yours to amuse yourself in.'

So much for charity mused Sean as he walked past the Gothic terrace houses with their extravagant facades that lined Northland Row, and came to the conclusion that his time as an altar server would soon come to an abrupt end.

A Dutch Auction

4

The week after the IRA attacked the Rosslea police barracks in County Fermanagh Sean read a report in the Tyrone Courier.

> "An RUC constable was seriously injured in the raid. Sergeant W. Robin Morrow (26) from Belfast was one of the youngest sergeants in the RUC. He had been asleep with his wife and two young children in the married quarters when he heard an explosion. He grabbed a Sten-gun and confronted the raiders. After a gun fight in which more than 100 bullets were exchanged they made off, escaping in two waiting cars. Two days later the Eire Government Information Bureau in Dublin announced that an inquest had been held on an unknown man who apparently died from gunshot wound."

What the article omitted to state was, that following the attack many houses in the town, belonging to known republicans, were raided by the police in a fruitless search for weapons and explosives. The disappearance of a twenty-eight year old lad called Frankie Keenan, who lived with his parents on the Coalisland Road fuelled speculation that the raid had been planned locally. Subsequent tension in the town overshadowed the Christmas festivities.

By mid-February of the following year when the mild westerly winds and the lengthening of the days hinted at the spring to come Sean took to walking out again along the Black Lough Road. The meadow lands that slipped down to the waters edge were still too wet and marshy to venture into. Wandering past the orlits at Lakeside Villas it crossed his mind that Billy Montgomery's bungalow would have made the ideal home from Eddie Tracey, whose unexplained absence continued to puzzle him. The political implications of this notion were to become a catalyst in a sectarian conflict that eventually engulfed most of the country.

Unemployment was always high in the town, particularly among young Catholic men. Many of them emigrated to England to look for work in the building sites and factories round London and the Midlands, particularly Manchester and Birmingham, while others joined the armed forces 'to see the world.' Those on the 'dole' gravitated towards the 'Boru' offices every Thursday to collect their unemployment money.

The 'Boru' was a red brick building located beside Holmes funeral parlour on the Ballygawley Road near the junction of several streets that ambled round the town. Set back off the road, its perimeter iron railings, hipped roof and classical arched windows gave it an air of authority, a

A Dutch Auction

fact not lost on the officials within, whose dealings with poor individuals was often far from charitable.

It was not until after school on Thursday the twenty-seventh of February that Sean heard about the audacious hold-up at the 'Boru' offices from his incredulous father. In fact over the next few days and weeks the Al Capone-style heist was virtually the sole topic of conversation, even the wireless news carried the story.

The police were out in force and roadblocks were set up on all the major roads, reinforcements were later drafted in from surrounding towns and detectives from Belfast arrived to supervise the operation. That night under the command of sergeant 'Soapie' Douglas, the 'B' specials began searching houses with some enthusiasm.

It appeared that when old Mr Monteith the manager unlocked the doors about eight forty a.m. he was greeted by three armed and masked men, who had entered the premises in the early hours of the morning. One of the burglars had somehow managed to gain entry through a small air vent high up in the back wall of the building by deftly clambering over the roofs of a row of houses in nearby Linfield Street without been seen or heard. The alarms were disconnected, the locks on the entrance doors picked from the inside and the two accomplices admitted before the doors were locked again.

'If ye don't do as I tell you, Monteith, I'll blow your fuckin head off, and that's a promise, you little pisser!,' snarled one of the trio, holding a pistol to the side of the terrified managers head.

In his statement to the police later the manager described how the men were all dressed in identical navy boiler-suits with knitted black balaclavas pulled over their heads, and two of them held Sten-guns in their gloved hands. He recalled that only the smaller stocky man with the pistol spoke, and his accent though local, betrayed some time spent in England, and though hooded he remembered seeing part of a deep scar running across the bridge of his nose.

Every Thursday morning at precisely 8.50am Mr Monteith unlocked the side door of the offices to admit an official of the Ulster Bank, who carried a canvas hold-all containing about £3,000, of used notes in modest denominations. This morning was no exception except that three unwanted guests grabbed him in the hallway, and bundled him and the manager into a store room before binding and gagging the petrified men.

At around 8.55am a black Austin Cambridge motor car was seen speeding down the Ballygawley Road which then turned into Newell Road at break-neck speed, with the thieves and their booty on board.

Speculation abounded about the 'Boru' job among the drinking fraternity in public houses like Stewarts in Irish Street, and among the crowds who patronised the weekly whist drives in St Patrick's hall at Union Place and even among the unemployed 'Fenian playboys' who hung around the square, smoking woodbine cigarettes.

A Dutch Auction

The get-away car was found an hour after the robbery in Cinders lane about a mile away, with its engine still running. It was presumed that the villains transferred to another vehicle and made good their escape. In the back seat the police found two loaded Sten-guns but not the revolver. Some time later they announced that a forensic examination of the bullet cases found outside Rosslea police barracks were identical with those in the Sten-guns.

Some citizens of the town wondered if the stolen money was used to fund a new life in America for Frankie Keenan.

5

Diagonal shafts of early morning light imprinted the oak floor of the sacristy with diamond shaped patterns as Sean reluctantly resumed his altar duties, in the first week of March. Taking a fresh candle he pushed it down hard into a waxy slot at the top of a heavy brass candlestick, as the sacristan helped Father McMahon with his vestments.

'Do you know something, Mark?' said the priest, busily tying the chord of his alb, 'I'm always amazed by the humility and generosity of the poor.' 'Is that a fact,' answered a tired-looking sacristan.'

Undeterred by the rebuff Father McMahon continued, 'Do you know a bloke called Eddie Tracey, by any chance?' 'Who?' squeaked Mark, biting his lip on hearing the name. 'Eddie Tracey,' repeated the priest, pronouncing the name slowly and with a little impatience. Father McMahon paused for a second, in the silence before saying, 'His father died about six months ago and he turned up out of the blue for the funeral. He's a bit of a jack the lad by all accounts I believe, though he hasn't been seen about for some time.' 'I've run across him all right,' muttered the sacristan and bending down lifted a bottle of red wine from a cupboard.

'He was fond of the bottle among other things,' continued Mark darkly, 'and as far as I know he's back living somewhere in England.'

The priest looked at his watch and gave an audible sigh for he was a few minutes early and in a reflective mood.

'It's such a spiritual thing you know, this whole notion of sin, repentance, salvation and forgiveness,' entoned the padre and glancing up at the crucified Christ hanging by the palms of his hands from a small cross on the stuccoed wall above him, he blessed himself solemnly.

Having poured a measure of wine into a glass cruet the sacristan turned towards Sean who was holding the candleabra, and putting his face close to his ear whispered, 'Are you going to stand there with your mouth open like a spailpin fanach or are you going to light the candles before next Christmas?' Adding in Irish, 'You little smart assed toe-rag.'

If Mark had bothered to look into Sean's eyes he would have realised that by now he understood these words of abuse.

A Dutch Auction

With a swish of his soutane Sean turned and retreated to the opposite end of the vestry to get the matches.

'Why did you ask about that Tracey fella?' asked the sacristan who had turned back towards the priest.

Father McMahon gently rubbed the side of the gold chalice like a child stroking the tail of a purring cat before answering, 'It's just that I opened a letter from him earlier, over in the parochial house, and in it he asked me to say masses for his deceased parents.'

With a wide smile the priest went on, 'The Lord works in mysterious ways, for inside the envelope was £200 in Ulster Bank notes, and all in fivers and tenners. What do you think of that for charity, Mark?'

The sacristan gave such a involuntary shudder that he almost toppled over. A stricken look appeared for a fleeting second on his pale countenance to be replaced by a darkening pool of controlled fury.

Tuesday being market day, the wide expanse of Ann Street that careered down from the Gallows Hill was filled from first light with carts of squealing pigs, braying donkeys with malicious yellow teeth, suckling calves, with bright frightened eyes and farmers from Gortnagola and Lisnagleer some of whom wielded bull-nosed ash-plants. Sean stood and watched Peter 'bad luck;' escape from a chained and padlocked straightjacket, as a small crowd of curious onlookers clapped half-heartedly. He fingered the sixpence in his trousers pocket and turning crossed the road towards Mac's fish and chip saloon.